THE BOY SHERLOCK HOLMES ✦ HIS 4ᵀᴴ CASE

THE SECRET FIEND

SHANE PEACOCK

Tundra Books

Published in Canada by Tundra Books,
75 Sherbourne Street, Toronto, Ontario M5A 2P9

Published in the United States by Tundra Books of Northern New York,
P.O. Box 1030, Plattsburgh, New York 12901

Library of Congress Control Number: 2009929061

Library and Archives Canada Cataloguing in Publication

Peacock, Shane
The secret fiend / Shane Peacock.

(The boy Sherlock Holmes)
ISBN 978-0-88776-853-8

1. Holmes, Sherlock (Fictitious character)--Juvenile
fiction. I. Title. II. Series: Peacock, Shane . Boy Sherlock
Holmes.

PS8581.E234S41 2010   jC813'.54   C2009-902980-4

We acknowledge the financial support of the Government of Canada through
the Book Publishing Industry Development Program (BPIDP) and that of
the Government of Ontario through the Ontario Media Development Corporation's
Ontario Book Initiative. We further acknowledge the support of the Canada Council
for the Arts and the Ontario Arts Council for our publishing program.

ONTARIO ARTS COUNCIL
CONSEIL DES ARTS DE L'ONTARIO

Design: Jennifer Lum

Printed and bound in Canada

ANCIENT FOREST
FRIENDLY

This book is printed on paper that is 100% recycled,
ancient-forest friendly (100% post-consumer recycled).

1 2 3 4 5 6 15 14 13 12 11 10

To Sammy,
the amazing Boy Peacock.

ACKNOWLEDGMENTS

Of the many books I read while writing this novel, several stood out: Liza Picard's *Victorian London 1840-1870: The Life of a City*, was a constant companion, not only for this case but for work on the entire Boy Sherlock series; Ben Weinreb and Christopher Hibbert's *The London Encyclopaedia* continued to be an immense aid as well; both Stanley Weintraub and Robert Blake's biographies of Disraeli were essential; as was Philip Callow's telling of the life of Robert Louis Stevenson. RLS, the great man himself, his insight into the human soul, and his marvelous novels, were a powerful inspiration. Lee Jackson, one of our great historians, whose *Dictionary of London* website (www. ⬛ictorianlondon.org) was s⬛ ⬛⬛⬛⬛ to me and many oth⬛ ⬛esearchers, personally ga⬛⬛ ⬛⬛ ⬛i⬛ time during the la⬛ ⬛⬛⬛⬛s of the creation of *Fiend*, wi⬛ ⬛⬛⬛⬛⬛⬛⬛⬛ ⬛⬛⬛⬛ ⬛⬛ation. I cannot omit the contribution of my father, Jackson Peacock, history teacher and brilliant thinker, who imbued me with a love of the past and has always been available for important discussions on pertinent historical matters. Thanks also to Kathryn Cole, my perfect editor. And to my family again, without whom I could not write a word. Finally, and most importantly this time, to Kathy Lowinger, who is saying "*au revoir*," but not farewell, and whom I will greatly miss, as will the whole publishing world.

CONTENTS

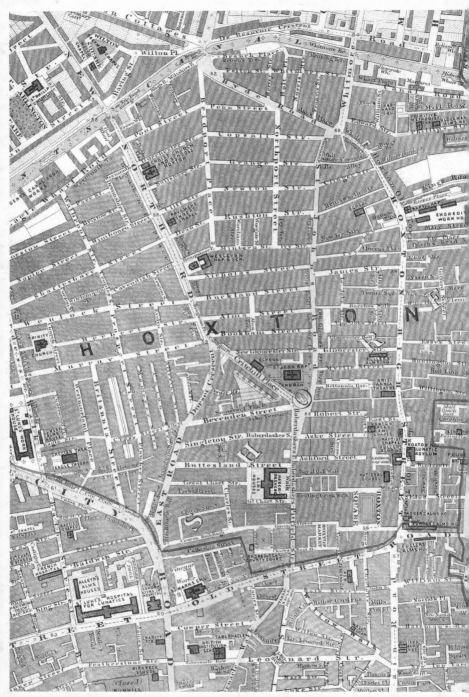

PREFACE

It appeared out of nowhere, leaping from a bank of the River Thames onto Westminster Bridge one dark, London night like a man endowed by the devil with superhuman powers. Two servant girls, walking arm in arm and frightened by the late hour, barely turned before it was on them. It gave a shriek and then did its deed, ripping one from the other and making off with her across the cobblestones, reaching the other side of the wide bridge in just a few bounds. There, it sprung up onto the balustrade, the limp girl in its arms, and jumped out into the night, its wings fluttering in the cold air as though it were a human bat escaped from the underworld. They struck the freezing water with a crash and the night was silent again, interrupted only by the frightened sobs of the other girl prostrate on the stones. Then she rose and ran as hard as she could, northward, toward Denmark Street.

"All the demoniacal force of the man masked behind that listless manner burst out in a paroxysm of energy."
– Dr. Watson in *The Adventure of the Second Stain*

1

ENTER TERRIFIED

There have been many late knocks on the old apothecary's door. Some even come, like this one, well past midnight. But this is a knock unlike any other. It is accompanied by a scream.

It is the last day of February 1868, a month after Sherlock Holmes' fourteenth birthday. The Prime Minister of England has just resigned and his right-hand man, the remarkable Jew-turned-Anglican, Benjamin Disraeli, is taking his place. The empire stands on the brink of an historic moment, but some are ill at ease. There are whispers in the streets and taverns, and in the mansions of Mayfair and Belgravia, that the brilliant, black-haired Hebrew with the romantic background and flirtatious manners – he of foreign race – cannot be good for England. It is almost as if a Negro had become president of the United States. Amidst all of this, the country is nearing a turning point: the lower classes are rising, gaining power, demanding more; financial markets are unstable; Irish terrorists, seeking independence from the empire, are bringing their violence to the world's greatest city. What will the future hold? Many fear that chaos is about to descend.

London is in a deep freeze tonight, but the tall, thin boy is warm and fast asleep in his wardrobe in the laboratory. The knock, though enacted by a slight arm and delicate fist, thunders through the shop. Sherlock gets to his feet in a flash. He pulls his trousers on under his oversized nightshirt, seizes his horsewhip, and rushes across the hard floor of the lab, sure that Sigerson Bell will be down the spiral staircase and by his side before he reaches the door. But there is no sound from the upper floor. In seconds, the boy stands poised at the entrance with his weapon, balanced on his feet, remembering Bell's instructions. He raises the whip to strike.

"Who is there?"

"Let me in, Sherlock!"

It is a girl's voice, but not one he knows. Darting to the latticed bow windows, he peeks outside. A young woman stands cowering there, looking behind her every few seconds, like a cornered fox at the end of the hunt. The boy can't make out her face through the thick glass and darkness, but it appears pale under a red bonnet and her coal-black hair. She seems to be alone.

Sherlock unbolts the entrance with a snap and the girl falls into the shop, gripping his bare feet with her frigid hands, as if she will never let go. She kicks violently at the door, slamming it shut on her second try. Sherlock locks it, bends down, takes her head in his hands, and lifts her face toward him.

"Beatrice?"

"Sherlock! Save me! It took 'er. A fiend from 'ell!"

Her voice is so charged with emotion that it still doesn't seem like hers. "Lock the door!"

"It's done. Calm yourself."

Beatrice Leckie, the plain-dressed hatter's daughter with the sparkling black eyes and porcelain skin, who has always seemed so interested in everything Sherlock does, is shaking like a leaf.

"Calm yourself," he repeats.

Sigerson Bell still hasn't stirred. It seems incredible. *How can he sleep through this?* But none of the old man's trombone-like snores are rattling the shop: all remains quiet upstairs.

Sherlock lifts Beatrice to her feet. She feels delicate in his embrace and folds herself into him, clinging like a child might grip its father. He is surprised at how wonderful this feels. In fact, he has to remind himself to set aside the warm feelings invading his senses – they are far too emotional. She has had some terrible experience. He must help her. *She* may be hysterical, but *he* cannot be. He has learned to remove feelings from his decision-making: feelings are always illogical. But it is difficult to still them at this moment. Beatrice Leckie is not without attractions. He hadn't noticed it when they were younger, but it's become evident lately. She isn't a stunning young lady like Irene Doyle, that blonde, brown-eyed, unpredictable dynamo who can draw one's attention across any crowded room. Beatrice is different. You have to look to really see her. And these past few months, much to his surprise, he has indeed been looking.

Control yourself. Help her.

He half-carries Beatrice into the lab and sets her into Bell's big basket chair just inside the door, then turns to boil some water with a Bunsen lamp and tort.

"Take deep breaths. No one will harm you here. I shall make us some tea. Then we will speak logically."

She nods her head. A very slight smile creeps across her lips as he turns away. Her big dark eyes glow as they follow him. He works at his task and in minutes has two flasks of hot black tea in hand.

"Try this."

Her fingers touch his and he nearly spills their drinks.

"Tell me what happened, calmly."

She reaches out and grips his hand in both of hers. They are warmer now, and soft too. He thinks he should pull back his hand, but doesn't.

"We were late getting 'ome – very late. It was shocking – 'ow late we were out."

Beatrice and Sherlock have known each other almost since they were born. She lives in her father's shop, directly below where the Holmes used to keep their little flat. But when Sherlock's mother was murdered and he came to live with Sigerson Bell, they were apart for an entire summer, the longest separation of their lives. When they met again at school, she seemed different – much more grown up, her figure filling out. She told Sherlock that he seemed different too, that he was taller and more worldly. After that, she started regarding him in a way that unsettled him.

About a month ago, Beatrice suddenly left school. Holmes didn't know why.

"I 'ave a job now, Sherlock, working as a scullery maid for a family in a good part of town," she tells him. "My friend and I – she is a maid in the kitchen and doesn't live in, either – we were asked to stay late because of a dinner they are 'aving tomorrow. We were so scared, Sherlock. It was just the two of us out alone. But I wanted to get 'ome, to 'elp Poppa. 'e must be so worried."

Beatrice's mother had died of tuberculosis a couple of years ago and her father soldiered on, doing everything, insisting that his only child continue as long as possible at school. Beatrice and Sherlock have an understanding of each other's pain.

"We walked very brisk-like, 'olding on to each other. We kept to the right thoroughfares, and no one bothered us . . . until we got to Westminster Bridge."

She begins to cry. Sherlock pulls his hand away.

"I should 'ave gone to the police, but I thought they might not believe –"

"Now, Beatrice. You mustn't weep. Tell me what happened."

"It was the Spring 'eeled Jack!"

The boy can't resist a smile. *What is she playing at?*

"Beatrice, listen to me. You were seeing things. The late night will do that to you. The Spring Heeled Jack is a fictional character, a Penny Dreadful shocker. You know that. The night was playing upon your imagination."

"Then where is Louise?"

"Louise?"

"My friend! She's gone!"

"I don't –"

"She was with me, Sherlock. I wasn't dreaming that. 'e took her! She's gone!"

She is sobbing now. Sherlock doesn't have an answer for such reactions from girls – never has had – not even from Beatrice. He can't answer the question either, something that always makes him uncomfortable. *She must be making this up.* Perhaps he will call her bluff.

"Shall we go out and investigate?"

"Could we? Bring a blade, or a pistol, if Mr. Bell keeps one. And you must take my 'and."

Not an entirely surprising response. I'll play along, thinks Sherlock. *Perhaps there will be something of interest in it.*

"No need for firearms. I shall bring this whip and we will be vigilant."

"Thank you." Beatrice beams and looks into his eyes as she takes his hand again. "Hurry."

"First," exclaims Sherlock, blushing and releasing himself as he rises to his feet, "I must tell the master."

He leads her across the lab and sets her on a tall, three-legged stool near the foot of the stairs, so she will be nearer him as he goes up to see his employer. She gives a start when she notices the skeletons hanging from nails on the walls between the teetering stacks of books and the pickled human and animal organs stored in the glassed cupboards. He retrieves his shoes, worn frock coat, and yellowing shirt from his wardrobe, ducks behind the examining table and puts them on. Beatrice turns her back. No need for his ragged necktie tonight, though he wishes he could observe himself in the mirror. But that would be too vain and unmanly in front of Beatrice. He tries to fix his hair as best he can.

"I shall be right back."

Sherlock rarely enters Bell's upstairs domain, and he wouldn't tonight either – he can accompany Beatrice himself – but the apothecary's silence disturbs him. Has his ancient friend expired?

Sherlock tries to keep the wooden steps of the spiral staircase from creaking as he ascends. He isn't sure why – he certainly isn't worried about waking the old man. It is as if he suspects something of Bell, and wants to surprise him. And why wouldn't he? The apothecary can be deceptive – he has been known to crouch at the top of these stairs and listen in silence to Sherlock's movements on the ground floor. The boy likes Sigerson Bell, in fact, might even admit that he almost loves him, but his master seems to have secrets too: there is always something that Holmes can't quite –

There is a sudden noise downstairs, a creaking sound like the front door opening.

Sherlock hasn't even gotten his head above the upper floor, hasn't yet observed the glorious mess that is Bell's bedroom and sitting room.

He freezes.

"Sherlock?" he hears Beatrice say under her breath. She sounds terrified.

Holmes retreats carefully. He doesn't turn around, just backs downward, retracing his steps.

My horsewhip . . . it's on the laboratory table.

"Keep quiet," he whispers, but his heart is pounding. *What if this is more than a story? What if someone, somehow like the vaunted Spring Heeled Jack of Penny Dreadful legend, has followed her here? Perhaps he murdered her friend. Dismembered her body . . . cut her in pieces. And now he has come for Beatrice.*

Sherlock reaches the laboratory in a crouch, crawls silently toward his friend, pulls her down to the floor and reaches up to the table. At first he can't locate the whip, but he searches around and then feels its hard, leather surface. He grips it like one might hold the reins of a thoroughbred before it is released at the Derby.

"Use your wrists, my boy!" screams Bell every time they practice . . . usually prior to the destruction of some portion of the laboratory.

Sherlock holds the whip aloft, slightly behind his shoulder to gather maximum force, and cocks his wrist. He silently moves into the front room. Whoever is at the outside door has no difficulty getting in. In fact, he (or it) seems to have a key! Sherlock can see the intruder's silhouette as it enters.

The boy leaps and snaps the whip, but whatever is before him is as quick as a panther. It vanishes momentarily, then is suddenly behind him, gripping his neck in a death hold. His spine is about to be snapped.

"My boy?"

"Mr. Bell?" answers Sherlock hoarsely.

The apothecary releases his apprentice, who drops to the floor, afraid that he is going to cough up the lining of his throat.

"My apologies."

"Quite all right."

The boy has indeed been growing lately and when he rises, his eyes are almost even with his bent-over master's. The old peepers betray a distinct look of guilt.

"Where . . . where were you, sir? It is well past midnight."

"Past two o'clock, I'm afraid."

"And?"

"And what? Oh. My whereabouts. Yes, well . . . out for a constitutional . . . quite . . . a constitutional. Taking some air!"

"At this hour, sir?"

"Could not sleep."

"I didn't hear you go by."

"Precisely. You never know what I might get up to, my boy."

It is a sentence meant to end the conversation. There is a tone of irritation in the old man's voice, which tells Sherlock that further questions are not welcome. Sigerson Bell is rarely cross with his charge and never cold. But the boy feels a breeze in these words. His master is trying to back him off. It is almost difficult to believe.

What is this about?

Bell moves toward the laboratory, then stops dead still, like a bloodhound that has sensed its quarry.

"We have a visitor? At this hour?"

Though Bell has yet to see Beatrice, he is somehow aware of her presence in the next room. As he floats through the lab door toward her, Sherlock notices that he is carrying something under one arm – it looks like clothing, though it is shiny, like a costume. It is green and black. The sight of it shocks him. He is thinking about the Spring Heeled Jack.

The old man is soon standing in front of Beatrice.

"My dear, you are trembling. Let me take your pulse and hear your tale. What brings you here at this hour? Are you an acquaintance of Master Holmes?"

He presses two fingers to the jugular vein on her neck. "Yes."

"And can you not visit him at more respectable hours?"

"It isn't as you think."

"I think nothing. I merely listen. You are nearing fifteen years of age, the daughter of a hatter, resident of Southwark but employed as a scullery maid in a wealthy part of town, beautiful and normally of good health, as fond of this boy as I . . . and deeply troubled by something that occurred within this past half hour."

"I was walking home with my friend Louise, when I saw –"

"She saw nothing." Holmes has entered the lab, his eyes still glancing down at the clothes under Bell's arm. He can see now that the old man is holding a bottle with black liquid in it too, and a large mask that could fit entirely over someone's face.

"She saw nothing? *Nothing* has increased the palpitations of her heart, dilated her pupils, and caused her to perspire on a February evening? I must meet this nothing. It is as extraordinary as Mr. Disraeli."

"She had a vision."

"A vision?" Bell turns back to Beatrice and regards her with a penetrating look. "Of what?"

"It was the –"

"She felt she was being followed."

"By what?" Bell isn't looking at Sherlock; he stares directly into the girl's eyes. It is a mesmerizing regard.

"The –" begins Beatrice.

"A thief, a rough of some sort who meant her evil, but she escaped from whatever it was, if it indeed ever existed. Miss Beatrice is, as you say, quite healthy."

"Did you see this . . . rough?"

"No, she didn't."

"Were you alone?"

"I –"

"Yes, she was."

"Sherlock," says Bell with irritation as he turns from the girl to the boy, "can she not speak for herself?"

"She is very frightened. I don't want to cause her undue upset."

"Quite."

"I was about to take her home."

"By all means."

Bell turns to Beatrice again. "And you are sure you did not get a good view of this fiend?"

She looks to Sherlock, reads the concern in those gray eyes, and stiffens her resolve.

"No. No, sir. I did not."

"Well, then . . . you must be on your way."

In seconds they are out the door. Sherlock would never think anything sinister about Sigerson Bell. And he isn't doing so now. He is just being cautious. He has seen many images of the Spring Heeled Jack in the Penny Dreadfuls. There are rumors that this fiend once truly existed and haunted the streets of London . . . back in Sigerson Bell's day.

It wore a costume. *It was green and black.*

2

"I have a confession to make," says Beatrice shyly, feeling safe and thrilled to have her arm through Sherlock's, as they walk south past Leicester Square and the magnificent Alhambra Palace Theatre on their way to Westminster. The square is quiet now. The glimmer of the gas lamps barely penetrates the dark, frozen night; only their footfalls and a few claps of horse hooves, a few mumbling voices and sudden shouts echo in the gloom. The last survivors of the glorious evening before, are straggling home or lying on cobblestones. A drunken tradesman stumbles toward them, his crooked nose leaking blood from a scrap. Sherlock steers Beatrice from the square and across a narrow street to the opposite foot pavement.

"'Fraid of me, is you lad! Come back and get some of what I 'as! I comes out at night and turns into the devil, me friend. The devil! That's what's inside o' me!"

Beatrice appears to be trembling, so Sherlock holds her a little tighter and doesn't notice the smile that comes over her face. She glances at him.

"I 'ave been following you, I 'ave," she says.

He stops. "You what?"

"It's of no consequence, honestly, Sherlock. I was just interested in what you were taking up your time with. That is, when you weren't assisting your master."

Sherlock's heartbeat increases. "You followed me?"

"Well, *following* might be stating it a pinch strongly, now that I think on it."

"Have you done this often?"

"No, no. No, Sherlock, not often. Not often at all. But –"

"But what?"

"I know you do police things. And I know it was you who 'elped Scotland Yard catch the East End murderer and the Brixton Gang and that you were some'ow involved in finding Victoria Rathbone."

"How did you –"

"No other boy could do such things. I'm proud of you, Sherlock 'olmes."

She is looking up at him with those big black eyes, leaning against him, warming him, gazing at him as if he were a great man. Sherlock Holmes considers himself to be beyond flattery. It is a thing born of weak emotions. But Beatrice Leckie disarms him. She isn't a deep thinker like Irene Doyle, but she isn't a fool, either. She wears her emotions on her poor sleeves, with none of the arts of feminine artificiality practiced by most English "ladies": the veneer of weakness, the fainting, the standing on ceremony, the clever games meant to gain things from men. He hates such dishonesty. Beatrice Leckie is a real girl, a real *person* – the personality you see on the surface is who she is. Mixed with her unadorned beauty, it is an intoxicating perfume . . . which Sherlock inhales.

"You know what I think," she says in a sweet voice, "I think you could be a great detective one day." This is almost more than he can bear, so he keeps quiet.

They pass through a near-empty Trafalgar Square, its fountains stilled, and head toward the heart of Westminster, the river now just a stone's throw to their left. The magnificent granite government buildings rise on either side of the wide avenue known as Whitehall; and Scotland Yard stands dark and mysterious near the water. Even the Lestrades will be home now, fast asleep. A few steps more and they pass Downing Street, where the day before yesterday, Mr. Disraeli, the Jew, took up his post as the leader of the United Kingdom.

The young couple is silent as they walk. Beatrice holds Sherlock's arm tightly, an acceptable thing to do in the street at night and her right, under the circumstances. Sherlock, despite himself, feels flattered to be the object of such affection. For a few moments they forget their mission.

But Westminster Bridge is nearing. Soon they feel the looming presence of the famous Abbey near it: the ancient, twin-towered Anglican church that holds the bodies of the kings and queens, and great statesmen and authors in its vaults. Even more imposing is the gothic complex that rises behind it: the Palace of Westminster, containing the House of Commons and the House of Lords. It is the seat of power of the world's greatest empire, perhaps the greatest the world has ever known. These days India, Canada, Australia, Ireland – and half the world, it seems – is kneeling before England's queen, the majestic Victoria . . . and her cunning new prime minister.

Whenever the boy is this close to Parliament, he feels a yearning in his chest. He never knows if it is fear or pride . . . or awe. The Clock Tower, Big Ben, is above them now. He looks way up and sees the dial's massive black-and-white face. His earliest memory is of being four years old and standing near here, viewing the tower's thirteen-ton iron bell that was cast in a foundry in Whitechapel, as it arrived on an open cart pulled by sixteen horses. The crowds were ten deep, the cheering deafening. His father the Jew held one hand, his mother the English lady held the other, his brother, Mycroft, by their side. As they walked away afterward, a man spit in front of Sherlock's black-haired, olive-skinned father and muttered that his mother was a disgrace.

Suddenly, Big Ben tolls. Its gigantic gong vibrates in their chests and seems to shake all of London. Beatrice cries out. Sherlock, startled at first, pulls her closer. Ben tolls again, and again. Three o'clock. There is something terrifying about those sounds, something like a warning in this time of the people's riots in Hyde Park and the Irish bombings in the streets. There are always Bobbies near the Parliament Buildings these days – Sherlock sees them now. One is looking toward him. Sometimes it feels as though the world is about to come to an end. *Could London, could the English Empire fall apart from within?*

The brown bridge is wide and imposing, made of cast iron and set on granite bases. A series of seven semi-circular arches marks its appearance, looking like monstrous, half-submerged eyes, staring down the River Thames. Gas lamps rise into the mist every thirty feet or so, casting dim spotlights into the murky darkness.

"It was over 'ere," says Beatrice as they step up onto the bridge, pointing toward the balustrade wall a few dozen steps away. "We were walking this way, our gaze straight ahead, not looking to either side, 'oping to get 'ome without any mischief befalling us. There was almost no one else about." Their shoes scuff along the stones.

She pulls Sherlock with her and then stops about a quarter of the way along the stone surface. "Then we 'eard it."

"Heard what?"

"I don't know if I can rightly describe it. It was like an 'iss."

"A hiss?"

She pulls away from Sherlock and turns toward Big Ben and the Parliament Buildings, rising above them in the night. She holds her arms wide and her face has an expression of horror, as if she were an actress emoting on a stage.

"Yes. And we turned. And there it was."

"The Spring Heeled Jack?"

"It 'ad been kneeling against the balustrade, and as we turned, it climbed up onto it . . . and spread its wings."

"Wings? Now, Beatrice —"

"It 'ad wings, Sherlock. I don't say that they were real, but it 'ad wings."

"What color?"

"They were black, as was the rest of 'im, but there was green too – green borders and streaks."

Sherlock thinks again of Bell's black and green costume.

"And . . . and 'e 'ad something like 'orns on his 'ead."

"Like the devil?"

"I know it sounds fanciful."

"So . . . it climbed up –"

"No. That isn't right. I misspoke. It didn't climb . . . it leapt."

Sherlock looks at the nearly five-foot high balustrade and runs his hand along its top, a surface only six inches across.

"He sprang up onto here? From a crouch?" Sherlock looks down more than fifty feet to the freezing water below.

"Yes, 'e did." She begins to weep.

He goes to her and puts a hand on her shoulder.

"It 'ad an 'orrible look on its face, a beet-red face, so angry . . ."

"A young man or older?"

"It was 'ard to tell, it was so distorted . . . but its 'air was black and its eyes . . . its eyes were black with red centers, and when it 'issed again . . . a blue flame came from its mouth."

"Now, Beatrice!"

"Don't believe me, if you want!" It is the first time he's ever heard her angry with him. "But THAT is what I saw! And if it isn't true, then where . . . where is Louise?" At this she puts her head into her hands and sobs.

Best to stick to the problem, thinks Sherlock, *try to solve it for her. And she indeed has a point . . . where is Louise? . . . Maybe Louise wasn't here to begin with.*

"How did he take her?"

"'e flew down from the wall at us, 'is wings widespread. I pulled back and so did Louise, but 'e seized 'er and lifted 'er up with enormous strength, carried her across the bridge to the opposite side . . . and leapt up."

"Leapt up onto a balustrade again? Carrying Louise? Are you sure?"

"And then . . . then . . . then 'e dove –"

"Dove off the wall? From there into the river?"

"I 'eard a sound like them striking the water. I 'eard 'er scream. It was nearly deserted 'ere and no one else was near enough to intervene. I didn't watch. I was lying on the ground. I should 'ave done more! But I just . . . just got up and ran . . . to you."

She throws herself into his arms, but he lifts her away and shakes her.

"Beatrice, control yourself. I know you can. You aren't weak and helpless. Now, you say you saw this, so you can help me shed some light on it . . . tell me exactly, and I mean EXACTLY where they left the wall when they descended."

She walks across the bridge toward the balustrade.

"It was . . . 'ere."

Sherlock wishes he had his father's spyglass. He follows and examines the surface. It is icy in places, but right where Beatrice indicates, it has indeed been disturbed. His heartbeat increases. He lowers his big, hawkish nose to the surface . . . and smells it like a bloodhound. He detects something. *What is that odor?* It's like rotting eggs. Then it comes to him. *Sulfur!* Bell keeps bottles of the yellow crystals in his laboratory and melts them into a red liquid. It has a distinct aroma. If one were to light it, it would indeed produce a flame that would look blue in the night. Anyone with an elementary knowledge of chemicals could dab sulfur in their mouth and pull the trick of having blue fumes emit as they spoke. The boy gazes straight down, then turns sharply back to Beatrice, his eyes sparkling.

"How big was this fiend?"

"I don't . . . I can't . . ."

"As big as me? Nine or ten stone?"

"A little taller I'd say, and 'eavier."

"Is Louise your size?"

Beatrice blushes. "We are about the same 'eight, a little past five feet . . . and she is 'ealthy, not too stout –"

"But a little stouter than you?"

She blushes again.

"I SAID . . . a little stouter than you? The truth, Beatrice!"

"Yes, Sherlock. Yes, I am a little slimmer."

"Wearing a bonnet, a servant's frock, no crinoline? Petticoats over a corset beneath? Like you?"

This time her face turns very red, but she answers. "Yes."

He turns back to the bridge, calculating. There is no ice on the river below. *Let's imagine this really happened. The drop is a little more than fifty feet, their weight about nineteen stone, their clothes heavy. The man leapt out from the bridge, may have held out his bat-like wings to cushion the fall. The river is deep here.*

"If they did this as you say, then they lived," he says out loud, "and they could have landed near the shore."

With that, he turns and walks briskly back toward Big Ben. Beatrice, after a moment's hesitation, follows on the run. In minutes, he is off the bridge and down the stones steps and near the river. A few small boats float on the water. The mudlarks, those who make their living from finding things by the shore, aren't out at this hour. Though the muddy shoreline is filled with stones and piers and wharfs of all sizes, there are bushes and brambles here and there. Sherlock spies a clump of them about even with the spot where the pair would have entered the water. Rushing forward, he sees two sets of footprints in the cold mud – a man and a woman's – leading from the water into the bushes. Five steps into the brambles, he finds a piece of black cloth, bordered with green. . . . Then he hears a moan.

"Over here, Beatrice!" he cries.

Sherlock hears something moving, scurrying away, about fifty feet or so down the shore. When he looks that way, he thinks he sees a shadow, rushing off. He wants to follow, but he must look for the girl – *that is what matters.*

It doesn't take much searching. He finds her, lying under the bushes, covered by them. Louise is insensible, but alive. Up ahead, the shadow has vanished.

"Oh, Lou!" cries Beatrice and kneels beside her.

There is a note pinned to Louise's dress, written in red on a large piece of white paper.

I HAVE RETURNED!

Sherlock pulls it off and stares at it.

No watermark. Careful writing, not rushed, almost feminine, a young hand.

A handful of frigid water scooped from the Thames and splashed onto the young lady's face brings her around immediately. Her green eyes, which go charmingly with her curly red hair, snap open and she starts. Surprisingly, she has no cuts, no apparent bruises, and rises to her feet without much trouble. Her purple dress and dark blue shawl have somehow already dried, are just a little damp. Sherlock frowns, glancing back and forth from the victim to the note. He throws his frock coat over Louise's shoulders and helps the girls up the embankment before seating them on a bench near the Parliament grounds. He crosses his arms and frowns at them again. Beatrice glances up at him, then back to her friend, then up again, appearing concerned about Sherlock's reaction.

"Do you two mind telling me what this is all about?"

"I don't know that I follow you, Sherlock. I 'ave told you what 'appened." He thinks he detects a slight tone of guilt in her voice, but isn't sure.

"What really transpired here?"

"It is as I said."

"Yes, Master 'olmes, it is as she said. And I is much obliged, I'm sure."

"How do you know what Beatrice said, Miss Louise?"

"I . . . I imagines it. I imagines she said what 'appened, true and clear. Beatrice is an 'onest sort, always 'as been."

"But you are not bruised from your mighty fall, you have no cuts, your dress and shawl are almost dry, you are not traumatized. It was easy to find you. This . . . this *note* looks like it was written on a desk in a clear hand, not scribbled by an agitated fiend. What could he have wanted with you? He did nothing to you. He simply fled."

"It ain't for me to judge what a devil wants. 'e 'as evil intent for women."

"Did he act out that intent?"

"Sherlock!"

"We must get to the truth of this, Beatrice. Did he, Miss Louise, act out his intent? Did he lift your dress and undergarments and brutally –"

"NO!"

"Then, why?"

"Louise said that it was not for 'er to know why such a fiend does as 'e does . . . and she is right."

"This fiend from a Penny Dreadful magazine? This figure, this bogeyman for the children of England, who has so many times appeared in drawings looking more terrifying and vivid than anything Mr. Dickens might imagine?"

"Imagine! Is that what you think? What could be our purpose?"

"That, Miss Beatrice, is for you to tell me."

"Why do you stand 'ere talking rubbish? This villain must be caught and punished! You 'ave friends at Scotland

Yard. You must go to them. We will come with you and make a full report."

"I wouldn't dare."

"I beg your pardon?"

"I would not dare confront Inspector Lestrade with such a fairy tale."

"FAIRY TALE!"

"Why did you do this, Beatrice . . . do I not pay you enough attention at –"

The slap that strikes his face is unlike any crack of a parasol he has ever received from Irene Doyle. Those were mere caresses next to this. Beatrice Leckie smacks him across his cheek with a stroke that comes out of nowhere and would have scored many centuries on the cricket field and brought all of England to its feet. Her strong working-class hands are small but not delicate – and there is passion in her blow. She indeed cares about Sherlock; he can feel that now. But whether there is hatred or love in her mind is uncertain.

He actually falls backward from the slap.

"Return to your master, you . . . you *little* boy! Go back to your dreams and your selfish ambitions! There is more to the world than you imagine. Leave us! We will get our own 'elp!"

There is nothing else he can do. Stunned, he leaves them sitting alone, seething on the bench under Big Ben. As he trudges home, he reconsiders everything he has seen and what the girls said, wondering if he might be wrong. But he can't believe that this "crime" was anything but a setup, created to draw him in. It was all too easy. Of the millions of possible targets in the city, why would this fiend strike *his* close friend, causing her to run directly to him? It is like an occurrence in a melodrama. But why did Beatrice strike him like that, why such absolute fire in her eyes, why was she so emotional about his refusal to help? There was real fear, real feeling in her anger, not just the reaction of a schemer found out. Was there really a Spring Heeled Jack on the loose in London? And why was Sigerson Bell carrying a black and green costume and sneaking around in the middle of the night . . . just when the villain appeared?

People aren't what they seem, not even friends. Everyone is a potential suspect at all times. Trust no one. That is the only wise thing that Malefactor has ever said. *But . . . Sigerson Bell, dressed up as a fiend?* It doesn't make any sense. After all, the villain had black hair, wasn't old. . . . But didn't the apothecary have a jar of black liquid in his hand tonight, and a full-faced mask? He might have performed some magic, transformed himself . . . or put someone else up to it. He thinks again of the blue flames coming from the Jack's mouth. Sherlock chides himself. *What I am considering is ridiculous.*

Then again, nothing about this incident makes sense. And girls *never* do, especially the ones who attract you. First there was Irene Doyle, now Beatrice Leckie.

Women!

He feels in his pocket for the villain's note. It isn't there.

3

Sherlock doesn't hear Sigerson Bell leave the shop later that morning. Bell is gone before the sun is up – before the boy awakes – and doesn't return until late at night. Holmes decides to keep a close watch over him the next day. It is a Sunday, the lad's day off, but he rouses at the same time as the old man, jumping up from his narrow bed in the wardrobe the instant he hears feet descending the spiral staircase. His master nearly falls down the remaining steps when he spots him. The apothecary adores his young charge, but has resigned himself to the fact that rising early is not one of the boy's strong points. He is a good lad, a hard worker . . . once he gets going.

They lock eyes and stare at each other for a long time, neither saying a word. Suspicion hangs thick in the air.

"My boy!"

"Yes, sir?"

"What is the occasion? You are out of bed prior to my descent!"

"I thought I'd turn over a new leaf. I plan to rise early from this day forward."

"And pigs shall fly from the rear ends of donkeys," says Bell under his breath.

"What was that, sir?"

"Not a thing, my boy, not a thing, just an expression of admiration. I embrace this initiative on your part. Shall you be fixing my breakfast as well?"

That is indeed his plan.

Everything seems to be almost normal with Sigerson Bell this morning. That is, as normal as things usually are around the shop.

As the curve-backed old man does his morning calisthenics of jumping jacks and running on the spot and hanging upside down from the rafters to send as much blood as possible to his brain and twisting himself into extraordinary poses that he holds for extended periods, Sherlock works away at the morning's repast: headcheese and prawns, to be washed down with buttermilk. The boy glances at the apothecary as he toils, thinking about what he knows of him. He is surprised to realize that when he actually considers it, the answer is *nothing*. Sigerson Bell is very good at learning about others, but rarely speaks intimately of himself. *Where did he come from? Who were his parents? Was he ever married? Who is this man with whom I have so thoroughly thrown in my lot?* Bell won't be attending church this morning; he never does, nor does he insist that the boy attend either . . . what kind of Englishman does that?

Their Sunday paper, *The News of the World*, will come later in the day, so they have no choice but to converse as they begin to consume their little feast. Bell, as usual, plows into it like a starving man, eating with his mouth wide open and head down. Sherlock regards him. After a while, the old man looks up, gobs of headcheese evident between his teeth.

"Is there something on your mind, Master Holmes?"

"I was just thinking."

"You were? Of what?"

"Of you."

Sigerson Bell swallows awkwardly, then retrieves a stained blanket that rests on a nearby stool and wipes his face.

"How very kind of you. I am well, thank you." He sounds disconcerted.

"I wasn't enquiring after your health, sir. I was just thinking –"

"You mentioned that."

"– that you have never told me anything of your past."

"Yes, that's true."

Bell resumes eating. Sherlock keeps staring. Finally, the old man sighs and looks back.

"I am not given to airing my autobiography. I think it best for others to know little of me. I function better as a question mark. I believe I treat you well, and that your knowing intimacies of my past will do nothing to enrich our relationship or our conversation. In fact, it may hinder them."

"But you know a good deal of me."

"I deduced much of it. And you volunteered the rest."

"You sound like an acquaintance of mine."

"Who is that?"

"One Malefactor."

"Ah, yes, the boy who operates the street gang. Thank you for casting me in such lovely company."

"Only in what you just said, sir, only in that. Malefactor also cautions others to hide their pasts."

"Well, in that, and in that alone, he has a point; though such secrecy is not for everyone. Some are given to displaying their lives, every intimate detail of them, for others to paw through. And yet, no one can ever reveal all about himself. Everyone has secrets."

"Would you object to telling me something about your past, sir, just something, it need not be intimate."

"Anything?"

"Yes."

A disturbed look crosses his face. "I had a wife . . . and she was a witch."

Sherlock can't believe how bitter the old man sounds. He has never heard him like this.

"Sir, might I be so bold as to suggest that that is rather unkind, and perhaps beneath you. No matter how difficult she might have been to live with, I do not think you should call her names."

"But she was a witch."

"Sir, I must repeat that —"

"She was an actual witch."

"I beg your pardon?"

"She was skilled in the ways of witchcraft. That doesn't mean evil. She was a God-fearing lady."

"But you said it in such an angry manner, Mr. Bell, that I thought —"

"She died when we were young." Tears come to his eyes. "She was just twenty-four, my boy, the most beautiful witch in the world. It was so unfair."

"I am sorry."

"You see what comes of speaking of intimate details! I told you before that I believe in the alchemical concept of optimism. I prefer to live in the present, neither looking backward, nor ahead. Enough!"

And that is all Sherlock can draw from Sigerson Bell that day.

But there is much that seems suspicious in the old man's actions. And Bell likely thinks the same of the boy. All day they play a sort of cat-and-mouse game, speaking less frequently than usual, constantly glancing at each other and quickly looking away, neither leaving the shop for a moment, despite the sunny late-winter day outside, both puttering away at seemingly unimportant duties – Sherlock cleaning up in places that appeared already quite tidy, the apothecary mixing solutions and mixing them again. For awhile, Bell turns to his skeletons, taking them down from their nails, gripping them in his arms and manipulating their bones, practicing his new art of skeletal adjustment, which he plans to use on unsuspecting patients with spinal ailments in the near future. He has come to the conclusion that had someone done something similar for him, he would not be as bent over as he is today.

Though Sherlock wants to keep his eye on Bell, he can't stand being cooped up forever. So, just after supper, he goes out for a walk. On his way, he spots Dupin, the legless newsboy, strapped to his wheeled platform, rolling along with his folding kiosk and leftover papers, as he leaves Trafalgar Square. The sight of him gives Sherlock an idea.

"Mr. Dupin!"

The ageless newsboy pulls over near the gray exterior of Northumberland House, out of the way of pedestrians. Sherlock approaches, and smiles down at him.

"Ah, Master 'olmes. What adventures is you in pursuit of these days?"

"These days, I am merely a student and an employee of Sigerson Bell."

"And a fine thing it is to be gainfully employed, even by that strange 'un. None of your snoopin' into criminal affairs anymore?"

"I am still a boy, Dupin, and I still have a great deal to learn. Best leave adult concerns to adults."

"And by the look in yer eye, guvna, you have something more you'd like to learn at this very moment."

"Do you recall the Spring Heeled Jack? Not from the Penny Dreadfuls. Wasn't there a real one at one time?"

"Indeed there was. Why do you ask?"

"I . . . am simply curious. Do you have any accounts of him in your notes?"

Dupin is not just a newspaper vendor but an expert in everything to do with the news. Among his few possessions is an extraordinary catalogue of almost every important event from the last few decades. It is referenced and cross-referenced. But his pages are only slightly better informed than his remarkable, retentive brain.

"That was long ago, you know, when I was a lad."

"Were you selling papers then?"

"I was. It was my first year, the second season of our Victoria's reign."

"Can you tell me anything more?"

Dupin regards him with a smile. "Why?"

Sherlock can do nothing but smile back. He fingers a shilling in his pocket. It is all he owns. Would Dupin give him the information for cash?

"Put your money away, Master 'olmes, but promise me this: if anything comes of whatever you is after, let me know the details."

"I fear, Mr. Dupin, that if anything does come of it, you will soon know as much as I."

Dupin grins. "Let me see." He slings his kiosk off his back, finds a wooden box and eases it down onto the hard foot pavement as if it contains the crown jewels. He begins flicking through its contents: uniform, neatly cut pieces of paper filled with information.

"1838 . . . A . . . H . . . S . . . Sp . . . Spring 'eeled Jack. 'ere it is."

He pulls a small sheet out of the box. "First struck late in that year. Both in London and in the vicinity, face like the devil, claws on 'is 'ands, red eyes, blue flames from his mouth –" Dupin can't help but laugh. "There were many reports that year and next and into the '40s, many imitators it seems, then reports fall off."

"What did he wear?"

"Wear?" Dupin gives him a questioning look, then

peruses the account again. "A costume . . . 'ad wings, dressed somewhat like a bat, black and green."

Sherlock swallows.

"Did they arrest anyone?"

Dupin reads again. "It seems . . . they brought in one man, respectable sort, but never prosecuted. 'pparently it weren't 'im. No one else was ever accused."

"Do they say how old the Jack was?"

"I recall that meself. I recall too, that it was almost exclusively women that 'e attacked, or just frightened usually, never badly 'urt any of 'em, though there were folks imitating 'im in other places that killed their victims. 'e was supposed to be, 'ccording to these ladies 'e scared, a man of nearly forty."

Sherlock walks back to the shop deep in thought. *It wore a black and green costume. And it struck about thirty years ago.* He doesn't know Sigerson Bell's age, but is guessing he is about seventy. This apothecary, with the chemical magic at hand to turn his eyes red and his breath blue . . . who hides his past, was *nearly forty* in 1838.

When Holmes returns, the sun has long since set, but Bell is still wrestling with his skeletons. In fact, as the boy enters, he is attempting to adjust a neck bone . . . and snaps the skull clean off the body. He utters a little curse under his breath.

"Oh, rat flatulence!" He turns to Sherlock. "I have had enough of this, and I am taking to my bed."

"But it is still early, sir."

"And I am fatigued. Is that all right with you, Sir Sherlock Holmes?"

"Yes, sir. I am sorry, sir."

The old man looks guilty. "Quite all right, my boy. That was my frustration speaking."

But Sherlock isn't sure he believes it. Once Bell is upstairs and apparently in bed, the boy makes noises downstairs, as if he is still working. At the appropriate time, he blows out the candles, turns off their gas lamp, undresses and gets under the blankets in his wardrobe. But he doesn't sleep. He listens. He hears a few horses and carriages go by outside, a few shouts in the street, but nothing from the floor above.

About four hours later, the pitch-black stillness of the shop is broken by a noise overhead.

Sigerson Bell is on his feet. Sherlock listens for the sound of his chamber pot being slid out from under his bed, for the familiar noise of pee spurting in irregular squirts into that vessel. But there's nothing of that sort. Instead, the boy hears the old man putting on his clothes! Moments later, he is coming down the stairs! Sherlock hears him putter through the lab, knock into something and still it. Then, there's a low voice.

"Dog flatulence!"

Silence.

The footsteps move again, through the lab, into the front room. The outside door squeaks open and closes.

4

Sherlock has his trousers, waistcoat, and frock coat on in seconds. He only glances into his little mirror, pats his hair into place in a rush. He gets out the door and spies the old man way down Crown Street, heading toward the river. Bell wisely avoids the dangerous Seven Dials and keeps going straight south to The Strand. Sherlock has to stay on his toes because the old man looks back several times, as if concerned that he is being followed. He has something tucked under an arm.

At The Strand, so unlike itself now because it is nearly deserted, the boy follows Bell as he heads east toward the Old City. They pass St. Paul's Cathedral, bare-foot waifs lying on its steps. Only the odd hansom cab passes, that signature London sound of clopping hooves now a lonely noise. It is still too early even for the working class to be starting out, and not a single milkwoman is yet in sight. Sherlock keeps his eyes open for shadows lurking down the alleyways. Malefactor and his gang could beat you, strip you, and clean out your pockets in a flash, unobserved at this hour. Respectable, sober folks know to keep from the streets in the early morning. Sherlock once had a sort of admiration for Malefactor, but now despises him. He would just as soon have him arrested as speak to him.

Up ahead, Bell seems to have no worries. He scoots along, bent over, never looking side to side, just occasionally behind. *He is fearless*, thinks Sherlock. But anyone as skilled in the arts of self-defense as he, is frightened of no man. In fact, the boy pities any thug who might try to accost him.

They pass south of Cheapside and the old man swings down to Thames Street next to the river. Sherlock can smell it. The Tower of London looms up ahead, looking ominous against the black sky. The boy's breath is evident in the cold night.

Bell stops suddenly, pulls the costume and mask out from under his arm as if readying it to put on, then scurries into one of those impossibly narrow streets in this ancient part of the city. Everything here is cramped, made for smaller people of a bygone era.

By the time Sherlock turns into the street, Bell has vanished. *He must have entered one of the buildings.* The boy begins examining them. They are block-like and jammed together, made of dark granite, gone black from centuries of grime and decades of soot. A few have business names on plaques, a barrister here, an exporter there. But one sign stops him in his tracks. It is unlike any other. There are no words, just a symbol containing a compass and a square joined together, with the large letter *G* in between. The door looks very heavy, curiously bolted from the outside. *Is it locked from the inside as well? If so, what a strange entrance.*

And he thinks it especially so when he sees a dim light through the cracks – someone is in there! Somehow, that person can lock and unlock the outside bolt from the inside. The door also features remarkable decorations, carved right into it – a whole series of pyramids each with a single eye peering out. Should he enter? Sherlock carefully draws the bolt, then reaches out and grips the handle. Suddenly, the door swings open and just as suddenly, he is on the ground. Someone has taken his legs out from under him with a deft move of a foot and an expert push from a forearm. His assailant stands over him.

"My boy?"

His master is astride him . . . frantically throwing off a black and green costume.

"Mr. Bell?"

"What, in the name of Hermes, are you doing here?"

"One might well ask the same question of you, sir."

The old man offers a hand and raises him to his feet.

"Yes, well, one might indeed, I suppose." Bell glances back at his costume, now lying in the entrance behind him, and tries to kick it through the doorway. "You are such a curious lad. Let us step away down the street here and I shall explain."

He is trying to get me away from the building. Sherlock looks above the doorway to the roof, searching for a clue to its identity. He sees nothing that helps, but then notices the costume, still lying on the threshold, not quite all the way through the door.

"By all means," says the boy. As the old man relaxes in response, turning his back to pick up the costume to throw it indoors, Sherlock makes a quick move, darts past Bell, and seizes the material. In an instant he is standing out in the street, several yards from the apothecary, examining it. It is mostly black, with stripes of green, but not really stripes – they are symbols of some sort, moons and suns, and more compasses and squares, more of those pyramids with eyes. Then he spots some lettering, written in a sort of Elizabethan calligraphy – *The Hermetic Order of the Sacred Dawn.*

"What?" says the boy aloud.

"I really wish you had not done that!" shouts Bell. He is advancing on the boy. He snatches the material from him and takes him by the collar. He drags him down the street and into an alleyway, looking right and left to make sure no one has followed them.

"I am required to kill you now."

"What?"

"That is what I am required to do."

"By whom?"

"By the Hermetic Order of the Sacred Dawn. You know of us now, you know our name, and you know that I am part of it."

"And I know you are the Spring Heeled Jack!"

Sigerson Bell's eyes look like they may pop out of his head.

"I'm what?"

"The Spring Heeled Jack!"

A smile spreads across Bell's face. "You have always been a strange one, Sherlock Holmes. But now you've done it. You have officially gone and lost your marbles."

"Say what you will . . . I am on to you."

"Yes, yes, I am a fictional character from a Penny Dreadful magazine. . . . You have caught me!"

"Why did you attack Beatrice and her friend? Or did you dress up someone else to do it?"

"Ah!"

"What do you mean . . . 'Ah!'"

"So that's what it was! Her *vision* was of the Spring Heeled Jack."

"Don't pretend you don't know. Don't pretend it is a surprise. I have caught you, red-handed. You have been using me, somehow. This was all set up. Why did you draw me into your employ in the first place?"

"Because I needed an assistant . . . and you are a wonderful young man, who thinks a little too highly of himself from time to time, full of troubles and indecision, yes, but a wonderful young man . . . who seeks justice."

"What? I thought you were about to kill me."

"I didn't say that. I said that was what I was *required* to do. But I would be as apt to actually do it as I would be to harness a thousand crows and use them to fly to the moon and back."

"But . . ."

"But nothing. Close your mouth and listen to me. I am not the Spring Heeled Jack. Neither am I Robin Hood, Goldilocks, or the Big Bad Wolf."

"But . . ."

"But nothing. I am a Mason."

"A Mason? You mean . . . someone who goes to meetings at Masonic Lodges?"

"Precisely. Most people know something of Masons, I am sure you have your own impressions. We are the descendants of the great builders of England and Europe, the architects of the world, creators of many structures since the time of Solomon's Temple, formed into lodges, all of us with philosophies and in pursuit of knowledge, seeking the Supreme Being together."

"Masons are secretive, aren't they? Once they're inside the walls of the lodges? You have secret codes, secret symbols, don't you? But aren't Masons just ordinary folk too . . . you aren't *terribly* secretive, are you?"

"Most lodges aren't. But we are. The Hermetic Order of the Sacred Dawn is a higher sect of our kind . . . a very high order. I am the highest ranking apothecary and alchemist, once the Worshipful Master here. I . . . I come from a long line of apothecaries, Master Holmes, my father and his father before him and on and on. There is a family story that the Bells once had the name Trismegistus and originated in Egypt long before we came to England, that we knew magic, real magic of the occult sort, not the stuff silly prestidigitators attempt on the London stages, sawing ladies in half and the like." He looks down at the green and black material. "This is what I wear when I enter the holy altar inside. Some outfits have masks with them too, black paint to mark our faces. Our order has associates all over Europe. We wield greater power than most can imagine. . . . And no one is to know our members' identities."

"No one?"

"No one. An outsider discovers us on pain of death."

Sherlock gulps.

"But I doubt the folks inside those walls," he waves down the street toward the building, "could ever kill another. I know I certainly couldn't . . . or maybe I could . . . but not you, Master Holmes, not you." He smiles at the boy.

"Thank you, sir."

"Your lips are sealed?"

"Yes, sir."

"Sealed with the best glue one could make from any horse in London? A triple promise with sugar piled on top?"

"Yes, sir."

"For life and beyond?"

"Absolutely. And I'm sorry about the . . . the Spring Heeled Jack idea."

Sigerson Bell laughs so loudly that he has to put his hand over his mouth to prevent someone from hearing and coming their way. "Give me a moment, let me gather myself. I shall put away the papers I had come to arrange and we shall walk home together. I want to hear more about Beatrice's vision."

An hour later they are strolling arm in arm along Fleet Street toward home. The sun will rise in an hour or two.

Now a few milkwomen are out, walking on their thick white-stockinged legs, their yokes over their shoulders, from which big pails dangle.

Sherlock tells Bell all about Beatrice's encounter on Westminster Bridge and what he found when he went to investigate. "So, in the end, it was nothing, sir. Especially now that my suspicions of you . . . and I must say again, sir, that, I am sorry . . ."

"Not at all, rather flattering I must say, at my age."

". . . it was just a young girl enamored of me."

"Oh! Is that what you think? You have a rather high opinion of your animal magnetism when it comes to the fairer sex, think you not? Do you really believe that a young girl would go to such lengths just to impress you? It seems unlikely to me."

"She is a nice girl, sir, very pleasant, but a simple one. I've known her since we were children. Her father is a hatter."

"I have seen this 'simple girl' with my own eyes, Sherlock. And I say, 'Beware.' She is more than she seems . . . as most women are. I shall tell you some day about my witch."

They part ways at Trafalgar Square, the old man anxious to get home to bed, the boy deciding to take a stroll down to Westminster Bridge before he heads back. He knows he won't be able to sleep. He has always been like that when something is on his mind – he could continue wide awake for a week, he sometimes thinks, if he were really intrigued by a problem. Perhaps he has been unfair to Beatrice, perhaps she and her friend were indeed accosted by someone on the bridge, nothing to really worry about – a lunatic of some sort – someone acting in a way that disturbed her impressionable female mind. Or perhaps it *was* a vision of a sort, a frightening image made by the lights in the London night and the fearful girls' imaginations. Perhaps Louise really believed it forced her toward the water: Beatrice fainted. He should have helped her, been more understanding.

When he arrives at the bridge, it is still pre-dawn, but there are people crossing toward the main part of the city, and a few going south. They are mostly working class, ready to start their trades early. But then Sherlock spots someone who stands out among these ordinary folk. He wears a bowler hat, and is examining the very spot on the bridge where Beatrice said she and her friend were attacked.

Lestrade.

5

It isn't the senior Lestrade, not the police inspector himself. It's Sherlock's friend, Master G. Lestrade. That narrow-faced lad, a few years older than he, is dressed, as always, in a sort of imitation of his father – checked brown suit with tie, brown bowler for a lid. The wisp of a mustache is just beginning above his upper lip. Though Sherlock respects him as a human being, he has yet to gain much admiration for his supposedly burgeoning detective skills. The only ability young Lestrade has that the boy cannot quite fathom, is his knack for sneaking up on others without notice. He has done it several times to Holmes, and it galls him.

Sherlock slips through the crowd and sneaks right up to the older boy. He comes within a few inches and then speaks softly into his ear.

"*It has returned!*"

Young Lestrade nearly leaps over the balustrade, into the river – his hat comes flying off and almost sails overboard too, though he catches it at the last moment, in an unintentionally comic move. Recognizing the voice at his ear, he gathers himself, straightens his suit, and calmly sets his lid back on his head, cocking it at a fashionable angle. He doesn't turn around.

"Master Holmes, what a strange thing to say."

Then he turns and smiles at the boy, their faces just a foot apart.

"Rings no bells with you?"

"All is silent."

"You are here for no purpose?"

"I am just on my way to the office."

"And I thought your family lived west of the city, north side, not south – curious that you would be out on this bridge. No need, really, on one's way to Scotland Yard."

"You know where we live?"

"There is a slight turn in certain vowels employed by many long-time residents of Hounslow. You and your father exhibit as much."

Lestrade sets his jaw tightly. "I thought I'd come out here and look at the river."

"Brown and smelly and cold on the second day of March? Lovely, that."

"Beauty is in the eye of the beholder."

"You have it with you."

"I beg your pardon?"

"The note. The one the so-called Spring Heeled Jack left last night."

Young Lestrade is barely able to contain his surprise, but he keeps his mouth from opening into a gape.

"Beatrice Leckie is a long-standing friend. She told me this yarn as well, brought me to this very spot last night, in fact. She must have taken the note to police headquarters. Is that how you ended up with it?"

The note had been written on a big sheet with big letters – Sherlock has noticed a bulge in Lestrades's left suit-coat pocket, one that such a sheet, folded many times, would make.

Lestrade says nothing for a moment, but soon relents. "All right. Yes, she brought it to Scotland Yard early yesterday morning. My father thought it nonsense."

"The only wise thing he has ever thought."

"I will thank you to never say anything of that nature in my presence again. You are not capable of even carrying his boots."

"I shall speak as I please."

"Very well – we have nothing to say to each other, then."

Lestrade turns back to the river.

"I found Beatrice's friend," says Sherlock, "one Louise, lying near the shore without a scratch on her. Her clothes were barely damp and she was not particularly cold, though her story is that she was carried through the air from this balustrade more than fifty feet into the freezing water of the Thames. The lettering on the note is not consistent with the hand of a madman. Miss Leckie, I must tell you, is an admirer of mine. She was seeking attention."

Lestrade wheels around.

"Who do you think you are, sir? You stain her name with that comment. I spoke to Miss Leckie myself, after my father politely refused to look into this. I found her to be believable. In fact, I found her a remarkable young lady."

Sherlock smiles. "And not without attractions."

"Step away from me, Master Holmes, or I may slap your face."

"You don't want to do that, my friend, believe me. However, I am sorry that I offended you. I have no quarrel with you, not at all." He turns to go, but then looks back. "Proceed as you see fit, Lestrade . . . against your father's wishes . . . but I warn you, you will be much more likely to catch a wild goose than the Spring Heeled Jack."

But Sherlock Holmes isn't so sure about all of this as he walks up Whitehall, back toward Trafalgar Square, and home. *If Beatrice was making this up, then why did she go to Scotland Yard with it? Surely she isn't so angry with me that she would make herself look like a fool to the Metropolitan London Police Force.* It would take monstrous chutzpah to go to them with a made-up story, especially one about a character from a Penny Dreadful come to life. *But if she isn't making it up, then why was Louise in the healthy condition he found her? She showed no signs of any attack. It is very puzzling.*

The sun is rising, the streets are filling. He should really get home and off to school. He isn't sure how much longer he'll attend. But he's a pupil teacher now, as well as top boy, and he needs to find a way to inveigle his way into a university. He must have higher education. So for now, his plans are to keep going to school; keep gaining the best grades at Snowfields.

Up ahead, Trafalgar Square is abuzz with activity, even more so than usual on a Monday morning. And it isn't just the number of people that seems different. There are Bobbies everywhere: Peelers on foot, Peelers on horseback, even Peelers up on rooftops, looking down. He sees several black-helmeted heads and blue shoulders on Morley's Hotel, more on Northumberland House. Crows are cawing. There is a palpable sense of danger in the air. *What's going on?*

Sherlock looks across the square, past the fountains, the statue of Charles I, the big monument to Admiral Nelson that rises up into the sky and sees a rough wooden stage in front of the steps to the National Art Gallery. It has obviously been pulled here by a big team of dray horses, all of which are still standing between the stage and a group of onlookers. He notices that some folks are carrying placards. He hears shouts, sees the crowd growing as he walks toward it, growing into a mob. Looking around, he notices other people actually running this way. Off to the side, down Pall Mall Street and on the other thoroughfares that go like spokes out from the square, he sees the Force gathered in large numbers, veritable battalions of police on horseback.

What is going on?

He sees the answer, then, standing on the stage. There, large as life, is the one and only John Bright, the most eloquent, the most bombastic, the most thrilling orator in the empire – and one of the most radical. He often speaks at Reform League demonstrations. When Mr. Disraeli, as Chancellor of the Exchequer, had pushed the latest Reform Bill through the House of Commons and made it law that twice as many Englishmen could vote as ever before, Mr. Bright had stood in the House and said it was not enough. There must be secret ballots, and every man in England must have a vote, he had said; we must become truly democratic, or the people will rise up and the consequences will be catastrophic. Chaos, he had said, will come to all our cities; violence will fill the streets.

A sensation goes through Sherlock, part fear, part thrill: it is curious how danger has two sides to it; how it can excite you and scare you at the same time. Over the last few years, demonstrations by Radicals both here and elsewhere in London have often grown violent. Last year in Hyde Park more than two hundred thousand protestors had stormed the fences and knocked them over, sending the police fleeing.

Today, the Force looks ready. They will fight back.

Sherlock spots another man on the stage, dark-haired and powerfully built like a rugby player. He wears a unique green suit with black stripes. He is looking at the crowd as if searching it for individual faces. There is something sinister about him. *Twenty-four or -five years old, Irish, by the cut of that Dublin-made suit. A man with an agenda, plotting something.*

"It's Munby!" shouts a man near Holmes.

So that's Alfred Munby! thinks Sherlock. *Controversial Reform League member, accused of Fenian connections, always denies any association with bombings, has had nothing proved against him. John Bright must be including him reluctantly.*

Sherlock rushes forward with the others, and pushes his way toward the front. He turns back to see how many more are coming, and something stops him in his tracks.

Malefactor.

He is at the edge of the crowd, leaning against a statue as if he owns it, his top hat cocked at a devilish angle, dressed as usual in his fading tailcoat, twirling his cane. His gray eyes are alert under a bulging forehead. There is a big grin on his face as he watches the rowdy scene. Arrayed on their rear ends on the stone ground against the plinth around him are his lower Irregulars, ten in number, nasty little boys dressed in eclectic combinations of stolen clothes; and right beside him, on either side, standing as he is and surveying the crowd, are his two lieutenants, dark little Grimsby and big, silent Crew. The latter, for some reason, has dyed his blond hair black.

There used to be a sense of amusement in Malefactor's face whenever he encountered Holmes, but when he spots him today, it is a very different look. It is hatred. They are now in open enmity. If looks could kill, Sherlock Holmes would be dead.

But almost immediately, Malefactor's gaze is averted by Sherlock's, who has noticed three particular people coming forward in the swarm of spectators approaching the stage. They are holding hands. It's a respectable looking middle-aged man with a walrus mustache, wearing a tweed suit, and a young lady, his daughter. Between them walks a little boy. Sherlock hasn't seen her for a few months. She is more beautiful than he remembers and grown up too, looking more like a woman than he can ever recall. But her looks are not all that have changed. The fashion of her clothes makes her stand out from the crowd. She wears a red linen dress without hoops or crinoline, so that it falls limply around her frame, showing her shape. The dress is of the sort the artists are wearing now, the kind the Pre-Raphaelite painters are depicting in their work, and it greatly surprises Sherlock. In a sea of bonnets, she wears a small hat, pinned atop her long blonde hair. Her brown eyes sparkle with intelligence. The sight of her fixes him to his spot. People jostle him, colliding against his shoulders as they run past toward the stage. But he just stands there, staring.

Irene Doyle used to smile a great deal, but lately things have changed: today her expression looks grim. Her jaw is set tightly and she barely hangs on to the little boy who steps along between her and her father. The reddish-blond child is dressed in a copy of Mr. Doyle's suit.

Sherlock is responsible for this family combination. The boy's name is Paul Doyle. It used to be Waller, nickname Dimly. The child used to languish in the Ratcliff workhouse in Stepney, going blind. But Sigerson Bell cured his eye infection. And Sherlock, who had discovered that the child was a relative of the Doyles, brought that fact to the attention of Irene's father, enlightening him in a private letter. Andrew C. Doyle, who had long ago lost his only son, adopted the waif within days . . . much to the disappointment of his only daughter. Paul, as Irene expected, immediately ascended to a position of prime importance in their household. It had given her another reason to turn away from Sherlock Holmes.

They spot each other. For an instant, her expression softens, but then those brown eyes flare and she looks away. When she does, she sees Malefactor. She stops. The rascal doffs his top hat. Her father looks over and notices why they have come to a halt. Irene is unsure of what to do. But then she waves back. Her father glares at her and pulls both his children away.

Andrew Doyle is liberal – very liberal. That is evident, not only in his many philanthropic ventures – help for the poor and downtrodden, his support of Radicals like John Bright and the forward-thinking John Stuart Mill (after whom he even named his dog) – but in the very fact that he is here today, amongst this rabble, bringing his five-year-old boy into a dangerous scene. Doyle and Son are obviously going to one day be a joint Liberal enterprise. But he draws the line at associating with people like Malefactor. Crime is no excuse, not even for the most desperate.

Malefactor places his topper back on his head and sneers at the philanthropist. Irene turns away from her father, gives Sherlock an icy glance, releases the little boy's hand, and raises her nose in the air. Doyle picks up Paul and makes his way toward the middle of the mob, Irene now trailing. They stop just ahead of Sherlock, not more than twenty feet away.

Despite her attitude, Holmes is thrilled. He has a clear view of her. He can stare. He senses that she knows he is observing her. Her appearance nearly makes him melt in the early March air. Beatrice Leckie is a mere crow next to this golden-haired nightingale. Really, there is no comparison. If Miss Doyle were on a London stage, not an eye would leave her.

Irene knows all of this. She has been more and more aware of her attractions as she has grown older and more womanly. She is changing both outside and in. And Malefactor, the bad boy she wants to reform, has been flattering and encouraging her for almost a year. As she stands there today, she is teasing Sherlock without his knowing. She has given him just the right view of her good side, the perfect pout of her lips.

"Good morning, friends!" shouts John Bright from the stage. A roar goes up and fills Trafalgar Square. It is a wave of noise, a call to arms. Excitement is instantly in the air. They chant his name. Munby joins in, shaking his fist, encouraging the crowd.

Bright is square faced and square built. Big mutton chops grow down his temples. He has a down-to-earth Lancashire accent, but there is nothing common about his eloquence. Despite his existence on the fringes of political life, his speeches are perhaps the best known in the land, the equal of Disraeli's. When England had entered the Crimean War more than a decade ago, Bright had spoken of "the wings of the angel of death beating throughout the land" and stilled the House of Commons as the members sat in awe. He raises his hands now and all is silent.

When he speaks it is not of rebellion, but of caution. He holds the massive audience in thrall, not with bombast and incitement to violence, but with carefully chosen words, political plans, even praise for the remarkably liberal Disraeli, a Conservative prime minister unlike any the nation has ever seen. He asks the people to give the Jew a chance, but to hold him and others to promises to continue to reform.

He finishes speaking and there is another roar from the crowd. Many turn to go, but he asks them to wait and hear a young man say a few words.

"I want to introduce Robert J. Hide, just twenty-two years old, but wise beyond his years, an English Alexander come to help his elders slice the Gordian Knot of the ruling classes' grip on our nation. I found him speaking in poor London boroughs and his eloquence, his passion, astounded me. This young man is, like all of you, England's future. Hear him!"

A striking man strides forward, purposely avoiding Munby, and takes Bright's spot at the front of the stage. Sherlock sees Irene's reaction to him. She forgets that she is being watched. She lifts her head and stares up at the stage, entranced.

Sherlock looks to Hide. He is indeed a handsome fellow, dark-haired, tall and well-built, fitting into his suit as if it were almost a second skin. His smile is beguiling, and his voice is pleasing.

The young man says little, but what he does say is cleverly put and charms the crowd. He finishes within five minutes.

"May I say in conclusion, that I hold with the great John Bright when it comes to our nation's future. We must not be violent or rash. We must work with Mr. Disraeli, and with Mr. Gladstone, we must roll up our sleeves and do this together, Liberal and Conservative, man and woman. It is my hope that one day, we shall all vote. And by that I truly mean *all*. Ladies, the fair sex, the true beauty of our empire, must vote with us, add their voices to our political world, and teach us how to be gentlemen with true wisdom in these days of great change. We must ALL go forward together.

"And so I say, good day to you! God bless you all! God Save the Queen!"

The cheer that goes up is not quite the roar that Bright received, but it is substantial, and Sherlock detects that its pitch is slightly higher than any other that morning. Looking around, Holmes sees women, both working class and ladies, glowing up at Robert Hide, their eyes still following him as he leaves the stage. Irene stands there too, looking after him as her father and stepbrother turn to go. Mr. Doyle has to touch her on the shoulder to get her attention.

Sherlock wants to follow Irene, but he shakes his head, trying to rattle good sense back into it. He must get going. He is late for school – if he goes now, then at least he can attend for most of the day. As he hurries across the square, he bumps into a small gathering of spectators. They seem to leap out of the crowd, causing him to run right into them.

Irregulars. They surround him.

"I am not pleased with you," growls Malefactor, coming out from behind them. "You knew I had a stake in the Rathbone situation. You cost me money." The two boys haven't spoken for a while. One has been making himself scarce, the other trying to attend to shop duties and school.

The older boy looks like he has grown an inch or two. There are wisps of sideburns spreading down his cheeks.

"My dear Malefactor, what a pleasure it is to see you." Sherlock looks about, hoping there are still Bobbies nearby.

"We are not children anymore, Holmes. I have plans. I will never allow you to stand in their way again."

"I –"

"DO YOU HEAR ME?"

"Might you speak up?"

"Match wits with me, Sherlock, and you will lose."

"We shall see."

A Bobbie trots by on a big black horse. Malefactor motions to his thugs and they move away from Holmes. Crew looks impassive, but Grimsby curses, disappointment etched on his face. He knows the apothecary's assistant is becoming skilled in some sort of fighting art that Chinamen use, but Grimsby is a street fighter, a killer-in-training, with no use for such nonsense – he fights dirty. He would love to get Sherlock alone in an alley and finish things between them.

"A lovely day," says Sherlock to Grimsby.

"Lovely, indeed," responds Malefactor with a winning smile, the Bobbie within earshot.

"Enjoy political rallies, do you?"

The Bobbie trots away.

"I enjoy chaos. If chaos doesn't come to London, I will bring it. Good day."

"The same to you."

"And remember what I said. If you ever involve your-self in attempting to solve any crime that has anything to do with me again, I will kill you, Sherlock Holmes. I promise you that. Until now, I have just been toying with you. But that's over. No more games."

Malefactor's eyes look cold and dead. Then he turns and saunters away as his gang runs off, Grimsby's giggle sounding across the square.

Sherlock is shaking – not something he would admit to anyone. He walks up St. Martin's Lane past the big stone church there, trying to compose himself. Before he has gone far, he sees a young woman sitting on a bench against a wall with someone leaning over her, his arm extended above her shoulder and his hand flat against the wall. They are deep in conversation.

Young Lestrade and Beatrice.

Sherlock tries to slip past. But she spots him.

"Master 'olmes?"

He stops. "Miss Leckie."

Lestrade sighs and turns around. He looks a little embarrassed, as if caught with his hand in the cookie jar.

"Master Lestrade."

"Holmes. I was just leaving. Good day, Miss Leckie." He doffs his bowler and walks away.

"Were you here for the demonstration, Beatrice?"

"Oh no, Sherlock, I don't believe in such things. I just 'appened to be nearby. I could 'ear that awful Mr. 'ide speaking. They say 'e is 'andsome, but I saw the side of 'is face when 'e was excited and don't agree. There is something sinister about 'im. I think 'e wants too much, that if 'e 'ad his way it would be terrible for England. The working classes need not *all* vote, that is nonsense, and neither, certainly, should women!"

Holmes smiles.

"I suppose I should 'ave told you that I picked that note from your pocket, and that I went to Scotland Yard with it. I am sorry."

"Not at all, Miss Beatrice. It is I who must apologize. I was a cad. You were frightened. I am sure that you did not invent what happened on the bridge. I hope the police will help you."

"They will not, but Master Lestrade 'as consented to look into things."

"That is a start."

"I have reflected on your reaction to what I told you the night before last and I understand why you would doubt me."

"Well —"

"No, Sherlock, I understand. What I told you would seem quite ridiculous, if you weren't there. I don't know 'ow you did not laugh out loud. But you were too polite."

"I did not mean to make light of your ordeal. Nor did I mean to suggest that you were in any way enamored of me."

"But I am."

Sherlock is taken aback. Those big black eyes look yearningly up at him. *A beautiful crow*, he thinks, *a beautiful crow indeed*. "Excuse me?"

"I do like you, Sherlock 'olmes." She glances down shyly, but then looks boldly up at him. "There is no use in denying it anymore. I cannot lie. I think you have become a fine young man."

The boy is tongue-tied. No one, since his mother was alive, has said anything like this to him. Beatrice notices that he is having trouble speaking and wants to help him, so she goes on.

"I am 'onored that you would think that I 'ave affection for you."

"Well . . . I . . ."

"And I am sorry to 'ave bothered you about all of this. Master Lestrade 'as many plans for 'ow he will investigate it. I am thankful for that."

"Perhaps . . . perhaps I could . . ."

"Yes?"

"Perhaps I might investigate just a little more too."

"Really?"

"Yes."

"And 'ow will you do that?"

"Will . . . will you be home this evening?"

"I certainly shall be, Master 'olmes," she says.

"Then might I see you at your parents' place of residence? At the shop? About nine?"

"You will be calling on me?"

"You could tell me what happened again, and I shall listen very carefully this time and see if there is anything of interest that strikes me."

"I 'ope something of interest strikes you, Master 'olmes, I do indeed. I shall see you at nine."

6

JACK IN THE NIGHT AGAIN

Sherlock Holmes wonders why he agreed to visit Beatrice Leckie. It was as if she gave him a chemical compound that drugged his senses, as if he didn't have the will to refuse. He figures it had something to do with the way she looked at him. But he told her he would call on her, so now he has to go. All day at school, he has been dreading this interview.

He tells Bell he won't be long and heads away. It is after eight o'clock and there's a pitch-black sky over the city. He crosses the Thames at Blackfriars Bridge and sets a course for his old neighborhood in Southwark. Dangerous London streets lie ahead.

Bravery is important to Sherlock. It is a British characteristic, seen not only in battle against the Spanish Armada and the great Napoleon, but on the playing fields of the nation's schools. It is also a characteristic that he knows he must have in order to confront evil. So, he always pushes himself to take courage. But tonight, he decides that following a direct route through the dark warrens and alleys toward his old neighborhood would be empty courage, a useless show that might end in his being attacked. There are many thugs and roughs who haunt this parish. He has time – he will take a slightly longer way, down the main thoroughfares, along Blackfriars Road and then up Borough High Street, before he turns off the main road to find the hatter's shop.

He tells himself that this decision has nothing to do with Malefactor or the Spring Heeled Jack.

But even in the slight flow of evening folks on the wider roads, he can't shake the feeling that something or someone is lurking behind him, down an alley to the side, or awaiting him up ahead.

By the time he approaches St. George's Circus, the loud roundabout near the big Surrey Theatre, he has had enough of taking this long route. Dangerous or not, he is sick of wasting his time, upset that he is allowing himself to be fearful.

He swings east down a narrow lane and moves past the stinking domes of the Phoenix Gas Works. Soon the street becomes darker and deserted and his heartbeat picks up. He keeps moving, refusing to look back, even when he thinks he hears scuffling along the cobblestones behind. He finds himself recalling his Bellitsu moves. Then, just before he reaches bigger, busier Bridge Street with its glowing gas lamps – a light at the end of the tunnel – he hears someone call out to him.

"Sherlock Holmes!" says a voice in a hiss.

He *has* to turn around.

"Chaos!"

The sound appears to be coming from above, on the rooftops. The boy looks up, scanning the uneven horizon of the haphazard stone and wooden structures, some abandoned, others sagging, all shadowy in the night. For an instant, he thinks he sees a human-sized figure up there, dark and bat-like, moving away from the edge of a building. *It appears to have black, pointed ears, like the devil.* The boy stands staring for a moment, frightened as much by his own fevered imagination, as by what he *might* have seen. He shakes his head to drive away the fantasy and moves on.

As he crosses Bridge Street, he is tempted to stay on it and resume a more circuitous, safer route to the hatter's shop. But he tells himself that is nonsense. He crosses the street, determined to walk straight toward his old haunts. He enters another lane. Almost immediately everything grows dark. There are no gas lamps here, just the dim glow of candles in one or two windows of the poor little homes and shops. He trips over something. No, it's *someone*, who moans. He leaps, jumping over the body, but when he regains his pace and surges forward, he sees a figure coming the opposite way, toward him.

"Ah, 'ere we is!" it cries. The voice is bizarre, a growl ushered up from an inhuman throat. Sherlock can't see the figure clearly. It looks as if it is wearing fur. He veers to the other side of the street, but it keeps coming at him.

"You can't run from me! I is more than one folk. I is everywhere!"

Sherlock can see him now, a beggar in bare feet, wearing rags, indeed made of furs, as if he were a caveman from prehistoric times. His hair is white on one side, black on the other: his face old and wrinkled, with calm eyes on the left, young and wild on the right. He has suffered some

horrible disease or injury. He reaches out for the boy.
Sherlock delivers a blow, the most severe he can muster,
right from the toolbox of the Bellitsu art, produced with his
left hand – his best – from a balanced stance, brought up
from below the chest, turning his hips as he follows
through. The beggar goes down instantly and for seconds is
dead silent. Then, he utters a groan.

Holmes begins to run. *Why did I hit that poor wretch?
Why am I running?* He wants to turn back and help the
beggar to his feet. But then he hears that voice again, the one
he heard in the other lane, calling to him from above.

"Sherlock Holmes! Chaos!"

He turns, glances up, and thinks he sees a winged
shadow, high on a building again. But he doesn't pause. He
turns back and sprints until he is all the way to Borough High
Street. Stopping there for a moment under a gas lamp, his
chest heaving, he changes his plans. He will give in: angry
with himself, he makes his way along this well-lighted main
thoroughfare. He moves quickly in the thin crowd under the
lamps – seeing tradesmen getting home late, couples out for
entertainment, men for drinks – past the shops and offices,
under taller buildings and awnings. By the time he nears
Mint Street, he has calmed down considerably.

But now, as he turns off the wide road, he must make
his way through a few more narrow lanes to get to the hatter's
shop. He shouldn't be afraid here: this is his old neighborhood of friendly buildings and little businesses. If anything,
he should be sad. When he last came here, he had held his
dying mother in his arms. But he can't stop feeling spooked.

He slips down a familiar little artery, his eyes alert. He has to be vigilant: the only light here comes from the main street's glow and a few little gas lamps behind windows. He gets down the first street, shoots along another and then turns onto his own.

His heart sinks when he sees the hatter's shop. Up above, in their little flat, he spots a dim light. *Someone has lodgings in their old home.* He knows it isn't his father. The boy has made enquiries and was told that Wilberforce Holmes is still living near the Crystal Palace in rooms provided for him by that entertainment complex's owners. It is for the best. Still, Sherlock wishes he could talk to him. He wants to hear his voice and pick his brilliant mind like in the old days. But he can't. Instead, he sends him letters, visits the Crystal Palace and watches him at a distance, sadly working with his white doves. Sherlock understands that he must stay away from his father, knows that his very presence would remind Wilber not just of his beautiful wife Rose, but of how his son, *this* son, Sherlock Holmes, caused her death.

There is a noise above. And this time, it's close.

Sherlock looks up. A human bat appears on the edge of the rooftop, right above the window in his old family flat. There is no doubt this time. The figure jumps, swooping down out of the black sky, knocking the boy over, thundering him to the ground. He smacks his head on the cobblestones.

Everything goes blurry. He tries to look up at it. *Is this the fiend's face?* In the fog, it appears incensed – complexion flushed, red eyes angry, spittle on its lips, blue flames coming from its mouth as it speaks in a deep, evil voice. Devil ears rise up in its hair, wings spread out from its body, and claws sprout from its hands. It wears a suit of some sort, striped black and green.

"Beware Sherlock Holmes! I bring chaos to London! Warn them!"

Is that what it is saying? He isn't sure. His vision is fading, growing dark. It stands over him, leans down, and rakes his face. He can feel the blood on his cheeks trickling toward his ears and neck. But he can't move. It is about to kill him and he is helpless, slipping into unconsciousness.

But then it rises. Before he blacks out, Sherlock can see its blurred image as if in a dream: it is wearing big, black boots with enormous heels. It stands grinning down at him for a moment, then springs halfway up the wall of the building, climbs to the rooftop and vanishes.

The boy lies immobile for a moment. But he's roused by a voice. Someone is calling him again.

"Sherlock?"

This voice is lovely.

"Sherlock!" He sees her porcelain white face, kind black eyes, black hair falling in ringlets down onto his chest as she leans over him, her face within inches of his. She smells of soap. *Beatrice.*

"You've been attacked! You're bleeding!"

"I am fine. It was nothing."

"But you're 'urt!"

"It was just a thug. He's gone."

"These streets are so 'orrible! Let's get you inside."

She puts his arm over her shoulder and helps him past the bow windows, toward the big wooden door of the shop. Groggy, Sherlock recognizes the old, familiar counter, the many hats – mostly black, some brown – hanging from hooks and on display. He remembers the smell of the mercury, the beaver and rabbit fur, and silk. He had worked here one summer or two, Beatrice often following him around, asking him questions, complementing every clever thing he said.

She takes him through to the back, to their home. It is warm inside, a fire burns on the hearth. There is no one else around – her father must be out. She guides him to a settee with a torn cover, pulls a blanket over him, then brings him a cup of tea that she's made for his arrival. In seconds, she is back with a warm cloth.

Though he takes the tea, he soon pulls off the blanket and sits up.

"I'm all right."

"But you aren't."

He puts his hands up to stop her from cleaning his cuts.

"Put your 'ands down, Sherlock 'olmes!"

He does so, immediately. She smiles at him.

"Now, sit still and we will clean you up."

She takes his strong chin in one hand and gently caresses the scrapes on his face. Miraculously, it doesn't hurt: the touch of a girl on his wounds is soothing. In minutes, he is put to rights.

"I came here to help you, not the other way around," says Sherlock. "I am not mortally wounded, you know. Let's talk about your troubles."

"Are you up to it, Sherlock? We could talk another night."

"Beatrice, I am fine! It was just a little knock on the head from falling and some scratches."

"It is curious," she says, looking at him.

"What?"

"That this rough didn't rob you. 'e didn't, did 'e?"

Sherlock feels in his pockets, finds his two shillings.

"'e didn't take your coat, your boots, your shirt, anything."

It is curious.

"'e just attacked you."

"He was simply a young tough out for a little pleasure. There are those in this city who find it in violence."

"He was young? Did you see 'im clearly?"

"Uh . . . no, I just assumed that. My error. I didn't see him at all. He attacked me from behind."

"You couldn't give a description to the police?"

"No, there's no need to."

"I'm surprised at you, Sherlock. Shouldn't they be told? If there is someone beating up people for pleasure, shouldn't the Force be informed?"

"There are many attacks like this every day, you know. I think your experience was more important."

She blushes.

"It is so kind of you to 'elp."

They settle in to talk. Sherlock gets her to go over the events of two nights past and listens as politely as he can, making it seem as though he is deeply interested. He acts the part of a concerned friend. His mother aspired to singing on the stage, a dream prevented by her class – but she had the talent of an actor in her veins. She often spoke to her son of how thespians exploit those skills. *It is all in your head. Find the core of the emotion you want to portray and embody it. You must become the person you want to be.* Beatrice feels his gaze on her, looking directly into her eyes, apparently fascinated. And to some extent, he actually is; and not solely because of her beauty. Something attacked him tonight. It was likely just a thug. Half-conscious, his head already filled with fevered ideas after his run through the dark alleys of Southwark, he likely imagined the assailant bore the face of the Jack. But he isn't entirely sure. And though he doubts there is anything to Beatrice's story – there are no conclusive facts – there are nagging concerns, feelings he can't entirely discard; it irritates him to be unable to dispense with them.

Then, something dawns on him. As he keeps his best fascinated gaze fixed on Beatrice . . . her words fade into the background.

What did that thug say? He kept repeating it. "Chaos." And what did Malefactor say to me? "I enjoy chaos. If chaos doesn't come to London, I will bring it."

Still looking intently at Beatrice, he tries to recall everything he can about the figure that attacked him. It was a good size . . . in fact, about Crew's size. He thinks of the shape of the big henchman's face and it matches; of his singular strength, his athletic ability. He thinks of Crew's high-pitched voice and recalls that this fiend was trying to lower his own. It had dark hair . . . and Malefactor's lieutenant has just dyed his black! And on top of everything, this assailant knew his name, knew where he was going, knew how to follow a victim, and knew the streets. The Irregulars have many tricks up their sleeves. This isn't a normal criminal act – it bears all the marks of a big brain behind the scenes. Sherlock remembers Malefactor's promise to kill him. Frighten him first, then murder him. Why did this "Spring Heeled Jack" attack Beatrice Leckie of all people . . . a friend of his? *He may have his answer.*

"Sherlock, are you listening to me?"

"Why . . . yes, Beatrice, of course."

"What were my last three words?"

"Uh . . . I can't quite –"

She giggles. "It's all right, Master 'olmes. I know young men 'ave much on their minds. Perhaps I am giving you ideas?"

"You are."

"I am?"

"Beatrice, I might know the identity of your Spring Heeled Jack."

"You might?" she looks genuinely surprised.

"And I may know how to catch him, too."

7

Sherlock returns to the hatter's shop the very next night. This time he crosses at Westminster Bridge and has everything perfectly timed. When he reaches Whitehall, he sees Beatrice and Louise out in front of him, coming into view exactly on schedule. Beatrice has a pocket watch and he has asked her to get there at precisely half past eight. Big Ben is silent on the Parliament Buildings in front of them. The boy feels for the horsewhip tucked up his sleeve. The girls are to walk slowly and make themselves conspicuous, as he is doing too. His heart is thumping. Crew is large and skilled, capable of murder. But he must trust the arts that Bell has taught him. That morning, before school, after explaining that a cat had scratched his face the previous night, he had asked for more fighting instruction, but of a particular kind.

"You want what, my boy?"

"I want to know how I would fight someone who

doesn't play by any rules, a sticky-wicket sort, someone who wants to kill me."

"Is there someone like this whom you expect to encounter shortly?"

"No sir."

"I, of course, am a blithering idiot and believe you without question."

"But sir —"

"You must seize him by the unmentionables."

"I beg your pardon?"

"His meat and vegetables, his cricket equipment, his private machinery!"

"Sir?"

"Seize them!"

The old man leaps at Sherlock, hand out like a claw, his face as red as a rose. Holmes turns and runs from the room.

"My boy! Come back! I intended to inflict no pain upon your actual person!"

Sherlock returns very slowly, peeking his head around the corner first, measuring the distance between himself and his excitable instructor, before he re-enters the lab.

"Take a deep breath, sir."

"Yes, my boy, I shall."

"Now, tell me exactly what to do. Just tell me."

Bell gathers himself.

"Murderous sorts are usually not cautious sorts. He is apt to make the first move, which is likely to be in the nature of a pounce or a charge. You must let your opponent come at you."

"I must?"

"Yes. Wait until you see the whites of his eyes, as it were!" Bell's eyes flash. "Come at me!" he screams.

"If I do so, sir, you must promise to not actually complete the maneuver."

Bell looks disappointed. "There is wisdom in what you say. I shall try. Come at me!"

Sherlock sighs and rushes at the old man who stands still until the boy is almost upon him, then he leaps to the side like a kangaroo and utters a shriek likely heard nowhere west of the jungles of Siam.

"KEE-AAHH!!!"

As he does, he brings the heel of his boot down like a sledge hammer toward Sherlock's leg, stopping less than an inch from shattering his target. Both combatants stand stock still, the boy aghast, the apothecary resisting temptation.

"Had I followed through with this blow, I would have crushed your patella bone, known to the masses as the kneecap . . . or snapped either the fibula or tibia, give or take a bone."

"I am thankful that you did not."

"Your enemy is now a one-legged man and in a rather extraordinary amount of pain. You have him at your command."

"Thank you, sir."

"Then!" shouts Bell. "You are on him!" With that, Bell

leaps upon Sherlock and slams him to the lab floor. "And you seize him by the –"

"Sir!"

The apothecary springs to his feet.

"Quite, my boy, quite. But you asked me what to do when someone is attempting to murder you. I have little time for murder, especially of you. Not my cup of tea! I live it out when asked about such a maneuver!"

It is almost as if Sigerson Trismegistus Bell once had to fight like that too.

"So I should –"

"The point is," continues Bell, leaning against the lab table now, "you must deliver a crushing blow that puts you to the advantage, then, rather than continuing to fight at a distance, you must take him to the ground . . . and fight dirty. Get your hands on him . . . and do him evil. And do it in a forthright manner, wherever you strike! I am sorry to have to speak this way, but you asked me about fighting a devil and I told you. THAT is how you do it."

Sherlock keeps Beatrice and Louise in sight, about one hundred feet in front. They are bait that he does not want to lose. As he watches his friend up ahead, he thinks about how she reacted to his plan last night. It wasn't what he expected. She seemed reluctant to be part of it at first.

"But you want to do this alone?" she had said.

"Yes. I have my reasons."

"Why, Sherlock? Shouldn't we bring the police, or at least Master Lestrade?"

"That won't be necessary. I have a feeling that this will be a personal encounter, anyway . . . a fight between me and someone I know."

"You do?"

"When it is over, you won't be bothered by the so-called Spring Heeled Jack anymore, I assure you."

"But this will be very dangerous. I saw 'im clearly – 'is face, 'is strength when 'e carried Louise – I know what 'e is capable of. You must bring 'elp!"

"I shall have three advantages. First, I have been taught self-defense of a most effective and violent kind. Second, I will bring a weapon with me. And third, he shall not expect to be attacked. I will have the drop on him, as it were."

"I still think –"

"Not another word. Bring Louise, take the same route home you took on the night you were attacked, arriving at Westminster at half past eight."

She didn't seem afraid, not in the least. That surprised him too. Her objections were solely to his being alone, for his safety. She is a brave and remarkable girl, who indeed cares for him.

He is alert as he approaches the bridge, eyeing the balustrades, the tops of the buildings beyond, the shadows.

He keeps rotating his gaze, left hand firmly on the horse-whip. Crew knows how to strike without warning.

There are a few dim lights in the House of Commons — as always, a sort of golden glow surrounds it. He wonders if Mr. Disraeli is in there somewhere, trying to keep England strong and safe.

It may be his imagination, but everyone he passes tonight seems to be on edge. There is tension in London. It isn't surprising. The newspapers have been carrying many lead stories about the potential for revolution on the streets of England — some adding that "the Jew" is not the right man for the job at this time in history. And today, right on the front page of *The Times*, no less, was another unsettling article that will have caught many eyes.

A faithful reader of the *Daily Telegraph* and any sensation paper he can find, Sherlock would not even have seen it had Dupin not drawn his attention its way.

"Sherlock 'olmes!" cried the old vendor, as the boy made his way through Trafalgar Square to school that morning. "There is something in *The Times* that I knows you will be wanting to see." He snapped open the paper and poked a finger at a headline.

DISTURBING ATTACK AT WESTMINSTER BRIDGE
A frightening incident, drawn to this reporter's

attention by an anonymous source, seems to have taken place on Westminster Bridge in the early morning of February 29. Two young ladies, names withheld to protect their reputations, are said to have been attacked by a fiend dressed as the Spring Heeled Jack. Though when first questioned about this, Scotland Yard denied it as "nonsense," another source momentarily gave it credence, and upon further enquiries, The Yard admitted that a complaint had indeed been made, but for "good reason" had not been taken seriously. The original report characterized the attack as a violent one, in which one young lady was temporarily absconded with, and languished, for a short while, near death. Now, this morning, comes several citizens' reports, communicated directly to the office of *The Times*, of a second attack in a Clerkenwell alley in the early hours, where a similar fiend menaced a young woman. At press time, the Force had not commented.

On his way home from school, Sherlock had waited outside Scotland Yard until young Lestrade came out the door. The boy followed him for at least a hundred yards. When the older lad paused, waiting for a chance to dart across the street between noisy omnibuses and hansom cabs, Sherlock had spoken softly into his ear.

"Read *The Times* today?"

Lestrade had bolted forward in front of a big coach, whose coachman shouted at him. "Do you WANT to be trampled, you idiot!"

Sherlock couldn't help but smile as Lestrade jumped back to the foot pavement and gathered himself.

"That's twice I've spooked you lately!"

"I am in no mood for jokes."

"I am sure. Were you the police source?"

"My lips are sealed."

"But they weren't yesterday."

"Hobbs, that fool reporter, devious man – you have his acquaintance, I believe – sought me out and asked me about the incident as if he already had the facts."

"Which he did, such as they are."

"So it seems. I didn't think to deny it until it was out of my mouth."

"One must always be dispassionate in police affairs, not let one's desires, shall we say, one's affections, alter one's –"

"Shut your mouth."

"Pursue cases because they are right to pursue, my friend, not because you care for anyone involved."

Lestrade sighs. "You are right. But I believe her story. It is worth pursuing."

"It must have been her who told *The Times*. She had to be the original source."

"No, she wasn't. I asked her myself, this forenoon."

"How is your father?"

"Livid."

"And how are you?"

Sherlock can't help liking the other boy, blundering youth that he is, but earnest and honest.

"I have been better."

"Keep your chin up. A solution may be at hand."

Sherlock is all the way across Westminster Bridge now. This is going to be a longer trip than the one he made last night. Beatrice and Louise can't take the narrow lanes and alleyways because that would truly make them vulnerable – too obvious a prey at which Crew could strike. No, the girls have been instructed to stick to the wider, brighter thoroughfares until just the right moment. Only then will Sherlock's plan put them into a situation so perfectly tempting that the villain will not be able to resist. And when he strikes, so will Sherlock Holmes.

As they leave the bridge, the wharfs, and flour mills visible on the south side of the river below, they enter Lambeth, east of Southwark. This is a mixed neighborhood filled with factories, theaters, slums, poor residences, and a few not so poor. Lambeth Palace, where the Archbishop of Canterbury lords it over the state religion is nearby, but so are hard-living tradesmen, dock workers, and Astley's Theatre. Sherlock keeps his eyes on the girls.

It takes them about half an hour to make their way along Westminster Road past the Female Orphan Asylum, through St. George's Circus, and up Borough High Street.

Never once do they veer off the main roads, and there is no sign of the fiend. The girls keep to themselves in these areas and move quickly. As they approach Mint Street, they turn into Sherlock's old haunts, down a narrow lane.

The boy rushes up to the corner and turns. The pair is just ahead, still unmolested. He pulls his horsewhip from his sleeve and grips it tightly. Crew will be well aware that this is the perfect place to strike. But the thug doesn't appear. Sherlock follows the girls down several small streets, even an alleyway, all the way to the hatter's shop. They do just what they were instructed to do, but no attack occurs. The girls stop at the hatter's door and turn back to Sherlock. Louise smiles shyly at him.

"I'm glad, really," says Beatrice. "You should not be doing this alone."

"I would have been fine. I was well prepared. I should have him in custody by now."

"Would you like to come in? Father won't be 'ome for an hour."

"There's no need."

"But –"

"I must be getting back."

Louise looks at Beatrice, disappointed for her.

"Don't you two ever walk home this late again; if you absolutely must, ask a gentleman to accompany you."

"Thank you, Sherlock."

"Yes, thank you, Master 'olmes," adds Louise.

The boy stomps away from the shop, head down, upset at this missed opportunity. He was sure it would work.

He is so intent on his thoughts that he almost misses it. He passes a short alleyway where a dark figure has its back turned to the street, struggling with something. Sherlock walks by, but then stops. *Did he imagine it?* The fog has started to settle in. He turns and peeks around the corner. There is indeed a figure there in the mist, tall and muscular, glancing out toward the street every now and then, as if he is doing something secretive. It takes a moment for Sherlock to realize what he is up to.

He is putting on a costume. It is black and green. It has wings.

8

CAUGHT IN THE ACT

Perhaps the easiest thing to do would be to jump the fiend as he leaves the alleyway, unprepared for an assault and unaware that he has been spotted. But as a burgeoning detective, Sherlock has a bad feeling about that. Something doesn't make sense here. Crew, near the top of the Irregulars' chain of command due to his unspeakable talents – trained by the incomparable Malefactor, shouldn't be making blunders. And yet, he has allowed himself to be spotted, to have his back to potential enemies. Malefactor would know of the report on the front page of *The Times*, and would assume that the Force might be on alert, that citizens were watching their neighborhoods carefully. And yet, here is Crew, visible and vulnerable, changing into his costume.

It's a trap, thinks Sherlock. Malefactor is likely nearby with his other weasels. They could kill him right now, while he is alone in a poor area with no one to observe his body being dumped into the Thames. Holmes backs away, presses himself against the clammy wall of a building, his breath evident in short, nervous bursts in the cool early-March evening. There are no gas lamps; they have expertly drawn him here. Malefactor, the genius, had considered what Sherlock would do, and had been dead right. The boy looks up to the roof of the buildings. He can't see anyone else . . . yet.

The costumed figure emerges from the alley. Holmes has a clear view of it now. It is definitely big and powerful, about Crew's size. It wears black boots with thick heels, a cape that gives the appearance of wings, dark ears sticking up in black hair, and something like claws on its gloved hands. It looks like the devil.

Sherlock lets it move away, but keeps it in sight. He glances back, forward, up. *Still no one else.* The night is nearly silent, only the distant sounds of ships' horns on the river can be heard.

The boy moves forward, cautious, sticking to the foot pavement, almost glued to the walls. The Jack is virtually retracing Sherlock's steps. The figure not only walks back up the street he just came from, but turns at the corner he turned at, turns at the next one too, then stops and looks down the next road . . . at the hatter's shop!

The area is somewhat open – a small, dirty square with a water pump at the center. Sherlock must be careful. But when the fiend walks straight toward the shop and then right up to the door, the boy has to set aside his caution. *What does Crew want with Beatrice? Or is it Louise? Or does he indeed want me? Is this the best way to draw me into the open where the Irregulars can strike, murder me in front of the shop, on the very doorstep of my old family home?*

Sherlock can't care about his safety anymore. It is time

to be brave. He must not let them win. "You have much to do in life," his mother had said to him as she died in his arms. *There is much to be done at this moment – two girls to be saved, a fiend and his vicious crime lord to be denied. I cannot back down!* Sherlock grips his horsewhip and runs toward the shop.

The villain hammers on the door. Then he leaps up, impossibly high, seizing the ridge at the top of the latticed bow window next to the door. He will be above Beatrice and to her side when she comes to the entrance.

Sherlock is running full out now, trying to observe peripherally as he goes, ready to be jumped by someone else from the side or behind. The Jack, clinging to the wall like a giant bat, is making a strange sound, growling deep in its throat. It is looking down at the door.

The boy is still ten feet away when Beatrice appears. The Jack leaps down, its wings billowing out, its roar cutting the night. She looks up and screams. Behind her, Louise faints and falls to the floor, hitting her head on the stone threshold. But Beatrice reaches out to fight her assailant. Still, he doesn't attack her. He lands a few feet from her and actually turns, as if to flee.

When he does, Sherlock Holmes is on him!

"Sherlock!" shouts the Jack in a voice the boy recognizes. It isn't Crew's.

Holmes is balanced on his feet, just as Bell taught him, the whip coiled, like a cobra ready to strike. He snaps it downward, wrapping the leather around his opponent's lower legs. Then he jerks the weapon back, toward his own hip. The fiend's feet fly out from under him, and he lands on his back on the pavement with a slap. Pulling the whip toward him again, Sherlock frees it from the groaning brute's legs and cocks it for another strike. Now for the coup de grâce. This next blow will finish his opponent, incapacitate him momentarily, and put him in so much pain that Sherlock will be able to bind his hands and feet with the whip. The boy is about to slash him across his face and eliminate his will to go on.

But this Spring Heeled Jack is as strong as legend tells, for before Sherlock can follow through, he is lying on the ground, halfway across the street. His enemy has sprung up and kicked him with both feet, right in the midsection, in a thrust that felt like it was powered by a locomotive. Sherlock tries to rise and as he does, hears Beatrice scream again. Shutters pop open in the adjoining homes.

The Jack is coming at him. The boy sees its face – red and angry, the horns sticking up through its hair. *It isn't Crew.*

Just as the fiend nears him, Sherlock gets to his feet. But his opponent seizes him . . . by the throat.

"The key" Sigerson Bell once said during a particularly stirring encounter in the shop, stripped to his tight-fighting leggings and naked to the waist, the white hair on his back so thick it would make a polar bear proud, "is to make the opponent's body move in directions it is not used to going.

Directions, shall we say, that it would never choose. For example . . . like this!"

With that, he had grabbed Sherlock by the tip of his smallest finger with his own thumb and forefinger and began to apply pressure. Immediately, the boy was flat on the ground, crying out for mercy.

"One can inflict an enormous amount of discomfort by applying extreme pressure to even the tiniest part of the human body. You see, my boy, your baby finger does NOT want to move in the direction I am forcing it."

"Sir, for the love of God, release me!"

Sherlock had never felt such pain.

"Oh! I am sorry, Master Holmes, I get carried away." He released the boy, who stayed on the floor, writhing in agony.

"I could also have gripped you here!"

And with that, he had reached down and grabbed the bare-footed Sherlock by the little toe of his left foot, holding it again between a thumb and forefinger. The pain was even more excruciating. The boy screamed so loudly that it would not have been surprising if the queen, three miles away in Buckingham Palace, had complained of the noise.

"I can make you do anything I want now. Stand up please!"

Sherlock leapt to his feet . . . or foot, bouncing up onto just one pin.

"I can make you go this way." He led Sherlock to the left, bouncing on one foot and crying out. "Or this way!"

He pulled the boy to the right. "I can make you fly to the moon, if I choose."

"SIR! IT'S ME. YOUR APPRENTICE! SHER-LOCK HOLMES!"

The old man released him. He looked a little disappointed. "Yes, quite right. I am getting too involved, too intense about this again. You are correct to chide me."

Sherlock had slumped into a chair.

"Now, if I seized you by the ear lobe, it would have the same . . ."

The boy had jumped up and hidden behind the laboratory table.

"Just tell me, sir, just tell me. No need for another demonstration."

"Quite right again." A smile came over his lips. "If you REALLY want to hurt your opponent. If you want to finish him quickly, do what I just did . . . to a BIG bone!"

The old man had showed him how.

As the Spring Heeled Jack grabs Sherlock by the throat with his right hand, intent it seems, on ripping it out, the boy does the opposite of what most thugs in London street fights would do. The Jack's arm is held straight out, stiff as a board. Rather than trying to simply knock the arm away, downward, Holmes grips his enemy by the forearm with his left hand, actually holding the Jack's arm in place, keeping it straight and held tight to the throat. Now, he has the big bone that Bell spoke of in exactly the position he wants it. Continuing to hold him firmly, Sherlock seizes the fiend under the elbow with his other hand.

"When you execute a maneuver, my boy, do so with the utmost violence!" Bell is fond of saying, his eyes alight. "No shrinking violets allowed!"

Sherlock pulls down on the Jack's forearm with his left hand and shoves up from under the villain's elbow with the right, moving his arm in directions it most definitely does not want to go. He does so as if he wants the elbow to fly into the air and sail over the River Thames. There is a loud *crack*, the sound of a big bone fracturing in two.

The Spring Heeled Jack's scream pierces the night. He is instantly on the ground, gripping his misshapen arm, moaning with pain, pleading with Sherlock Holmes for mercy.

Down the street somewhere, they hear a loud, piercing whistle.

"John Silver!"

Beatrice has rushed forward and is standing beside Sherlock, looking down at the injured villain. Louise has arisen from her faint and is walking toward them too, holding her head.

"John Silver?" repeats Sherlock. It is indeed that boy, though not really a boy anymore. He lies in a heap, holding his arm, his clothes now obviously a crude costume he has made – his hair oiled up to look like it sprouts ears, his face smeared with coal, a ragged black cape with green stripes over his shoulders, black gloves on his hands, with nails protruding from the fingers.

"I am sorry, Beatrice," cries Silver, "wery sorry. I was just tryin' to scare you. I liked you so in school, but you'd never looks at me!"

"And you thought this would make me do so, John Silver?"

"I knows that some girls, they like the bad 'uns, the scary 'uns. I is big and strong, and I can handle meself. Lots of girls, they like that. I thought I'd scare you, then come back and offer to protect you. I thought maybe I'd tell you later that I was the Spring 'eeled Jack . . . maybe you'd . . . kind of like that too . . . maybe?"

"Then you don't know a thing about me, Master Silver."

The big lad, his face white with pain, drops his head and grips his arm, then looks up to Sherlock. "You've learned to fight, you 'as, 'olmes."

It has been more than a year since Holmes last encountered John Silver, the former bully of Snowfields National School. He was the biggest boy there, and the most athletic, with muscles bulging through his soiled clothes, his feats in the little stone schoolyard extraordinary – he could leap like no one else. They had grappled once, on the cobblestone ground outside the school near the London Bridge Railway Station, Silver a full eleven stone in weight, pinning thin Sherlock down, spitting on him, slapping him in the face, calling him Judas the Jew, humiliating him in front of his classmates.

But that was long ago. And much has happened since.

"Yes, Silver, I have learned to defend myself. I have done quite well . . . for a Jew."

"I am sorry, Sherlock. I didn't means nuthin' by it. I never did, really." The big lad, now seventeen years old, begins to cry.

"You are a fool. But if Miss Leckie and Miss Louise will accept your apology, so shall I." Beatrice and Louise nod. "I must tell you, however, that what you have been doing these last few days is against the laws of our nation, and your prank may have had more serious consequences than you imagined. Get to your feet!"

Silver struggles to his pins, gasping with pain, gingerly holding his broken right arm with his left.

"Last few days?"

"Close your mouth. I heard a police whistle at the moment I fractured your arm. I have no doubt that a Bobbie or two will be here in moments. I will stand just a short distance up the street, in the shadows. It is foggy enough now that they won't see me. You will stay here, in this square with Miss Leckie and her friend. You shall not touch them, speak to them, or even look at them . . . I will watch you! When the police arrive, Miss Leckie will inform them that you attacked her, just as you did Miss Louise on Westminster Bridge, leaping down tonight from the roof of her father's shop, but you fell and fractured your arm, and also sprained both your ankles, so badly that you could not escape. You shall admit to both of your assaults, the one on the bridge and the one tonight. As you see the Force approach, you will pretend to be crawling away, your ankles injured. Lie down."

"But it wasn't me, Master 'olmes! I promise you. I just got dressed up tonight, first time! I reads about it in the paper . . . and I thought of doing it. It wasn't me that first time on the bridge, nor the other time! I just did it tonight."

"Sherlock," says Beatrice, "perhaps 'e is telling the truth, perhaps —"

Sherlock steps toward Silver, a menacing look in his eyes. "Get down! Get down or I will crack your other arm the way I did the first!"

Silver immediately slumps to the cobblestones.

"Miss Beatrice is indeed a lovely lady, too lovely to be near the likes of you. She is kind and forgiving. But you sir, must feel the full force of the law against you, or you shall do something like this again. Take your medicine, sir, go to jail, contemplate your life . . . and change it!"

"But . . ."

"I will be in the shadows up the street . . . watching you."

"Sherlock," says Beatrice, "I will tell them what truly 'appened. I will tell them 'ow brave you were, 'ow —"

"If you care for me, Miss Leckie, you will say nothing of the kind. I have had it with seeking notoriety. It is enough for me that justice has been served tonight, that this fool is off the street. Perhaps there will be a day when I feel differently. Good night. I am glad that you are safe, and that your safety has been assured into the future."

She glows at him. He fades into the fog and hides in a

doorway up the street. He must admit that it feels good to do it this way. In a sense, it makes him an even greater hero. But he shakes off that inflated notion. *Justice.* He has protected Beatrice the way he should have protected his mother, and Irene Doyle. That is what matters. Moments later, three Bobbies rush past, and Beatrice calls out to them.

Sherlock Holmes walks slowly back through Southwark and over Blackfriars Bridge toward Denmark Street. He feels strong and powerful on the dark footpaths, not fearful in the least. *I was wrong about the Jack being Crew, that's true, but in the end, I found the villain.* He takes all the back arteries, the little lanes. The case of the Spring Heeled Jack . . . solved.

There are many ways that people get pleasure from life. Perhaps this is the way he will get his. Sherlock Holmes allows himself a grin.

9

"**S**herlock!" exclaims Sigerson Bell as he rushes into the shop the next morning. "You're name is in the newspaper!"

The boy had come home from Southwark exhausted, dropped into his little wardrobe, closed its doors, and fallen fast asleep, dozing soundly with nary a dream or a concern (a rare thing for him), completely satisfied with his night's work – he had done the right thing in every respect. But the old man had thrown open his doors like something earth-shattering had to be announced. Sherlock rose up so suddenly that he slammed his head against the wardrobe ceiling.

"In the newspaper? Which one?"

". . . In both of them, I am afraid."

Afraid?

The shop receives two daily papers: the serious-minded *Daily Telegraph* and Bell's gift to Sherlock, the sensational *News of the World*.

"And were I a wagering man, I would place great sums on the probability that your name is in every publication in London this morning."

Sherlock had planned to have a sort of a victory chat with the old man this forenoon – laying out in detail his heroic actions and his solution to the *Mystery of the Return of the Spring Heeled Jack*. He hoped to have his explanation all finished and the apothecary's deep admiration before he made his way to school. But this appearance in the morning publications more than gives him pause, as does Bell's less-than-joyous attitude toward it.

"Let us have a look." The boy reaches out for the paper.

"Perhaps after school?" Bell snatches it back.

After school?

Had Beatrice or Louise or maybe even John Silver not kept their word and informed the police, who had then informed the papers about his solution to this sensational crime? But if so . . . why isn't Bell proud of him?

"Before you read the article – after school – let me congratulate you upon the arrest of at least one culprit representing himself as The Spring Heeled Jack!" Bell summons a huge smile and pats Sherlock violently on the shoulder. It is a rather poor piece of acting.

"One culprit? What do you mean by that, sir?"

The apothecary sighs. "Perhaps you should, indeed . . . read the article. It is on the first page." He hands the paper to the boy and sits at the table, unable to face him.

Sherlock reads.

IT STRIKES AGAIN

The Spring Heeled Jack has struck once

more. This time in Knightsbridge, near the homes of several cabinet ministers. This attack was indeed a frightening one, the villain appearing out of nowhere and knocking a coachman unconscious before pulling two terrified ladies from the carriage, manhandling them, and sending them to the ground. Both fainted and the Jack was looming over them like a monster when Constables Balfour and Cummey, who had heard the ladies' screams, came sailing up Piccadilly to aid them. The fiend, however, took one look at the men in blue and vanished, lighting onto a water pipe and ascending it like a monkey before gaining the rooftops and disappearing into the night. The Bobbies recall a man dressed somewhat like a bat, wearing a cape, with devilish ears, and having claws on his hands. He wore large black boots as well and seemed to possess great bounding ability. Upon recovery, the victims described the assailant as well-muscled and spoke of their hearts fluttering at very high rates and the perspiration on the villain's face actually dripping onto their own. They reported too that he had fiery red-eyes and something blue emitted from his mouth as he cried out in a deep voice. He shouted the same thing to them as he wrote on a note he left behind, described in blood-red lettering.

"CHAOS!"

Sherlock can't believe what he has just read. *Was it Crew? Or a new Jack?* But despite this surprising news, there really isn't anything in it that Sigerson Bell wouldn't want him to see. Is there? Bell doesn't know yet that he caught Silver last night, doesn't know that he thought he had this case solved. Or does he? The old man has his back to him, but he is a mind reader of extraordinary power. Somehow, he knows the boy has paused.

"Read on," he says, waving his hand.

The boy turns back to the remaining paragraphs.

Curiously, an amateur imitator of the Jack was also accosted last night at about the same time the real one struck again in Knightsbridge. This was a mere boy named John Silver, who dressed himself in a Jack costume and attempted to frighten one of the young ladies who had been attacked by the real villain a few days past. Silver has revealed to the police that he knew her in school and had affection for her. In the course of the brief investigation, it was also discovered that a friend of the young lady's, who had been following her too, came to her aid, breaking Silver's arm.

Members of the Force were quickly on the scene, thinking at first that the genuine Jack had struck again. A red-faced Inspector Lestrade, who came rushing to this location from Knightsbridge, emerged from interviews in a hatter's shop nearby and, though usually tight-lipped about police matters, addressed reporters at length. He named the other boy who was in the school-boy scuffle – one Sherlock Holmes, a poor apothecary's apprentice.

"This young brat, of Jewish origins, fancies himself an amateur sleuth, and has previously interfered with the Force. I doubt we will even charge Silver – he simply needs some stern attention to his derriere with a switch. There are too many amateurs about these days, both representing the villains and the side of justice. We will countenance no further interference. And I will assure the London public this . . . we will catch the true fiend and catch him soon."

"I am sorry, my boy," says Bell in a quiet voice.

But Sherlock isn't feeling any sorrow for himself. He is simply seething. He is angry that he did not effectively keep his name from the news, and boiling about that ferret-faced Inspector, that buffoon who fancies himself a brilliant detective. And above and beyond everything, he is upset that he should have been in this situation in the first place. After having the good fortune to solve the Victoria Rathbone case, he had vowed that he would stay out of police work until he became a man, until he had worked diligently enough and long enough at his education, his fighting skills, his general maturity to face danger in the cause of justice, to truly help others wounded by villainy, and actually begin the job of avenging his mother's death. He had told himself that he would only enter the fray if a case sought him out and he had absolutely no choice but to pursue it. There had not been much probability of that.

Instead, he had allowed himself to get caught up in a little concern, a personal one, brought to him by a dark-eyed girl with a pretty smile and a deep admiration for him. He had been flattered into action . . . and look what had occurred, look what came of such *feelings*. He had been publicly humiliated, and his nemesis, that boob Lestrade, had been the agent of his embarrassment. On top of everything, a real fiend, a terribly dangerous one, veritably from the pages of the Penny Dreadfuls, is on the loose in London . . . and he hasn't a clue who it is. The account in the paper frightens him: this "Spring Heeled Jack," he is sure, will soon be murdering his victims. Beatrice, it seems, has been telling the truth all along.

Sigerson Trismegistus Bell stirs on his stool at the lab. He turns and faces his beloved apprentice.

"You have only one option now, you know, my boy."

"And what is that, sir?"

"You must come out of retirement."

10

Sherlock Holmes tries to be a regular boy the next day. He attends school and listens carefully. He is the only one in his form, learning at a level, he has been told, that no other student has ever reached at Snowfields. Sherlock also puts in his two hours as a pupil teacher instructing the little ones, helps the Headmaster clean up afterward, and is the last one out before the big wooden door on the ground floor of the big brick building is locked. He will clean the apothecary shop when he returns home. It will be a satisfying day's work.

But during all of this, a tension, a burning excitement, builds inside him. A devil wants out. At times he even notices his hands shaking. So far, he has resisted the volcano inside. Sigerson Bell *may* be right. Perhaps he should pursue this fiend. *Perhaps.* Feelings welling inside him are telling him as much. But they are *feelings*. He must be prudent.

As he walks home along Snowfields Road and heads past the large railway station, he spots London Bridge up ahead and sighs. He likes to play little mental games to keep his brain exercised. *How many steps is it from here to the bridge?* He is training himself to judge distances – there may be a day when it will come in handy. *Nine hundred steps*, he estimates. Then he adds to his game. *If I am able to travel that entire distance without once thinking of the Spring Heeled Jack, I shall resist him for good, leave him to the police to catch. That's a vow.*

At step number two hundred and twenty-two, his head cast down and his thoughts disciplined, he is interrupted.

"Sherlock."

A lovely voice.

Beatrice Leckie and her friend Louise appear in the crowd of faces coming toward him, having just crossed the bridge from the city, heading south. She has obviously taken this route to her father's shop in order to intercept him, either rushing here at the end of a short day, or during a late tea time.

"Miss Leckie."

She catches the less-than-enthusiastic tone in his voice. "Sherlock," she says, "I did not volunteer information about you to the press."

"But you did not keep quiet when asked, either."

"No." Her head lowers. Then she looks at him, her eyes large. "I am glad to have met up with you today."

There is something about her that prevents Sherlock from being angry with her. "And I, you," he says. He turns to her companion. "Good day, Miss Louise."

"Good day, sir." Louise actually curtsies. As the boy looks at her, it occurs to him that he knows nothing of this new friend of Beatrice's, not even her last name. *Who is this person with my schoolmate? She was the victim the first time, not Beatrice. Perhaps she was the only target.* Sherlock has never considered what her game might be in all the goings-on about the Spring –

He stops his thoughts.

"It is a fine day, ladies." And it is: cold but clear, with spring in the air. "I am afraid that I am in a rush. I am needed at the shop." If he'd had a hat, he would have tipped it. He starts on his way, but Beatrice reaches out and actually takes him by the arm, gripping him firmly, as if to hold him there. Pedestrians move past, taking notice of the bold young lady, standing so close to the young man that her chest almost touches his.

"I want you to find him."

"I have no idea to whom you are referring." He begins to pull away. He just has to make it to London Bridge without hearing that name, just six hundred and seventy eight steps and –

"The Spring 'eeled Jack."

His shoulders slouch. And what happens next doesn't help the situation. Beatrice slides her hand down to his hand and holds it tightly. Louise blushes, smiles, and speaks in a soft voice. "We is in danger, Master 'olmes." Her tone appears calculated to sound weak and vulnerable.

"Nonsense."

"I 'ope you are correct," says Beatrice, squeezing his hand as he tries to get it loose, "but Master Lestrade, who 'as been spending time comforting me, says that the police are absolutely certain John Silver acted *only* last night."

"That was not your fault, Master 'olmes," adds Louise,

"thinkin' that you 'ad nabbed the real 'un. I am sure that Master Lestrade could 'ave done no better 'imself."

Sherlock feels the color rising to his face.

"And I *know* 'e couldn't 'ave!" declares Beatrice, still holding Sherlock's hand tightly.

"This is a police matter."

Beatrice turns those big, pleading eyes on him again. "It is clear that the villain who attacked us in Westminster was the one who assaulted those ladies in Knightsbridge, isn't it? 'e is lunatic, a murderous one, and 'e knows who we are, how we come 'ome at night, perhaps even where we live."

"Then you must be careful, take a different route, go with a gentleman, and come home earlier, as you are doing now."

"I'm so afraid, Master 'olmes," says Louise and a tear plops onto her cheek.

It is as if they are working together.

"There is no evidence that this fiend will strike at you again. There are four million people in London, so probability suggests that you are quite safe."

"But 'e was reported near our shop past midnight last night," says Beatrice.

"He was? By whom?"

"It was a couple of lads, out carousing."

Sherlock smiles. "Hardly reliable."

"Master Lestrade says they are. 'e came at dawn this morning to the shop, and interviewed them – roused them up from their beds. 'e tells me 'e believes them."

"And that he must protect you?"

"Yes. 'e 'as convinced his father to post a man out on Borough High Street nearby, and 'e promises to stop in every night, too."

"He would."

"Pardon me?"

"How nice of him."

"I wish it was you . . . protecting me. I know the police will do what they can to catch this villain, and that they have been embarrassed into action, but I also know that the inspector thinks it is no more than someone pulling pranks, that the fiend isn't really dangerous. Master Lestrade told me as much. But I've seen the Jack – 'e will murder someone . . . maybe us!"

"Come now Beatrice. As I said, there is little evidence that –"

"There's something in the afternoon papers today," says Louise, "about it appearing *again*, somewhere else, last night. We 'eard the newsboys shouting out something 'bout it trying to attack some ladies again. It was in Brixton, wasn't it Bea? That's so close to us!"

"I know that Inspector Lestrade thinks you are out of the way now," says Beatrice, "because of what 'e said about you in the papers. But if you were to become involved in this, I think it would change everything. I think 'e would turn London upside down to find the Spring 'eeled Jack. I know 'ow 'e despises you and what you've done. You've made 'im look a fool . . . Master Lestrade 'as told me too."

It almost makes Sherlock feel proud.

"London should be on fire with fear! Your involvement would ensure it!"

The boy is surprised at the expression in Beatrice Leckie's face. It is lit up, her eyes actually angry. But she looks guilty the moment the words are out of her mouth. "I grow a little 'ysterical. I am sorry. But I'm . . . terrified."

Louise puts her hand on Beatrice's shoulder.

"That is natural, Miss Leckie," says Sherlock. "You and your friend were assaulted. No wonder you are fearful. But . . . you have Master Lestrade. He will look after you."

And with that, Sherlock loosens her hand and walks away, up toward London Bridge.

"You don't need to find him all by yourself, Master 'olmes! Just let Lestrade know that you are interested! That would be enough!" shouts Beatrice.

"The inspector thinks 'e's shamed you!" adds Louise, "that you don't 'ave the courage to 'elp anymore!"

Holmes is trying not to listen, waving his hand as he moves away. *There are many crimes in London*, he tells himself. *I cannot solve them all. I cannot be swayed by emotions. And I am still just a boy. I was fortunate before – all of this is beyond me. I should only act if I have no options.*

He walks slowly home, telling himself that the vow he made to investigate the Spring Heeled Jack if he heard or contemplated the villain's name before he reached London Bridge was just a child's game and that Beatrice and Louise's fears are unfounded – they are safe. He reaches Fleet Street where the newspapers are published. He likes the atmosphere here.

There is always a bustle: the omnibuses and hansom cabs clattering, the newsboys shouting.

"Leaping Jack loose again!" one calls. Sherlock sees a few pedestrians take papers from this particularly loud little vendor, flipping coins his way, hungrily reading the front page. But most people are simply rushing along as if they have important places to go. He smells the constantly lingering aroma of burning coal, the refuse, the perspiration, the perfume. There is no fog late this afternoon, and he can see all the colors of London: the black and brown horses, big black-and-white signs, the gray, shoeless children, the red and purple dresses and flowery hats, the pale faces, all as clear as day. But as he gets to The Strand and then moves toward Trafalgar Square, it seems as though the crowd is thicker than usual. There is a commotion up ahead. Past Northumberland House, he sees that people are rushing into the square from the streets. That is certainly abnormal at this hour.

Sherlock crosses the street and peers over the heads of the crowd, the top hats and bonnets, and sees why.

Robert Hide. He is standing on another crude stage near the north end of the square, in front of the stately National Art Gallery. It is Thursday, just three days since his exciting appearance here with John Bright. *Two Reform League demonstrations in one week?* Sherlock has never heard of such a thing. Perhaps Hide has organized this on his own.

The boy makes his way through the crowd to get near the front. He passes all sorts – working class, middle class, and aristocrats. Then he spots her. *Irene.* She is at the front, wearing another of those loose artistic dresses, orange this time, watching Hide with a look of admiration. In a sea of people in varying headgear, she alone is hatless. Her golden hair, hanging loose, glows in the sun.

Hide is pacing, the way a pugilist does before he enters the prize ring, as if holding something in. Sherlock notices Alfred Munby, dark and muscular in his green-and-black suit, heading toward the stage, but he is intercepted by a Reform League man who motions to him to stay off the podium. He glares up at Hide. But the young orator doesn't notice. He is glancing down into the front of the crowd now, regarding his admirers. His expression changes from a frown to a glorious smile. Several of his fans reach up to him. He bends and moves along, touching hands . . . one of them is Irene's.

Hide straightens and faces his audience. His brown eyes are glowing.

"My fellow Englishmen!" A big cheer rises, louder than any he received before. He is indeed a growing star. "I will take up little of your time this afternoon, but I thought it necessary in these extraordinary days — nay, in this extraordinary week — to speak with you once more." He thrusts his arms into the air. "Because we have a new man now fully at work at Number Ten Downing Street!"

Some cheer and others groan.

"Mr. Disraeli is a leader unlike any other. He is brilliant and open-minded, a seeker of consensus. Some say though . . . that he is erratic and unpredictable! An opportunist!" Hide frowns and holds his hands in fists.

"Here! Here!" shout some.

"I do not! He is my leader as he is all of yours, and I bow to his guidance." He places his hand over his heart. "But . . . he takes office at a time when trouble continues to dog our nation, when trouble seems to be growing. The markets are poor, the trade unions are restless, and the need for further reform is absolutely necessary." Hide begins to pace again. "Can he take us further? Change our nation, douse the flame of discontent rather than throw coal upon it by turning his back on us?" As Hide reaches the end of the sentence he is shouting and the crowd is cheering. He pauses. Silence descends. Irene stares up.

"I believe he can. But I believe that it is up to us, to you and you and you and you," he points at individuals in the crowd, ". . . and to me . . . to push him. We must remind him every day that England is not the way it should be – yet. We must all vote, ALL of us; we must have a secret ballot; we must pay our tradesman more; we must tax our wealthy citizens more, those who have so much!"

A cheer goes up through part of the crowd. Others look around nervously.

"But be not afraid, London, even in these fearful times, this fearful week. Chaos . . ." he pauses and laughs, "as this heinous Spring Heeled Jack fellow is telling us . . . is NOT here. Chaos shall never come to London or to our government as long as I, for one, have a BREATH TO BREATHE!" He punches the air with one of his big fists and everyone cheers. The sound fills the square and spills into the rest of the city. He lets it continue, posing for a moment, his handsome face upturned, holding that fist in the air, his bicep bulging under his neat, pin-striped suit, his slim waist evident as his coat pulls open. Sherlock sees Irene staring up at him, her mouth open.

On he goes, calling for change, but standing behind the government and the "good sense of sober people." He ends with a flourish. "Chaos comes only when fear consumes us, when fear runs loose in our streets, when fear trembles the tower at Westminster and freezes Big Ben, when you, the people, allow fear into your veins! We shall not . . . we shall not . . . FEAR! We fear . . . nothing!"

For an instant Sherlock thinks he sees Beatrice, moving through the crowd near the front, and disappearing behind the stage. But that is impossible – he has just seen her south of London Bridge. To get here, she would have had to double back. *Am I thinking about her too much? Am I becoming attracted to her?*

The applause continues for many minutes after Hide finishes. He leaps from the stage and the crowd folds around him. Some embrace him, others shake his hand. Sherlock stands watching, noticing Irene trying to get nearer the charismatic man. Soon, Hide moves Holmes's way and it is only when he is almost upon the boy that Irene finally reaches him. Hide sees her, looks enchanted – *who wouldn't be* – and shakes her hand like a gentleman. As he turns, he is face-to-face with Sherlock Holmes.

"Hello, sir," Hide says in a confident voice and takes the boy's hand. Most people of higher social standing than Sherlock don't even acknowledge him. They see his threadbare suit and waistcoat, his old boots, polished so often that he's created holes and turn away. But this famous young man smiles at him. "Thank you for listening," he says, looking right at the boy. If Sherlock Holmes can do anything, he can judge character. He can tell that Robert Hide means what he says.

As the boy turns away, someone jostles him, and he is pushed into Irene Doyle. Their faces almost touch. For a moment they are held by the crowd, eyes inches apart. Irene, for once, isn't frowning at him.

"Hello, Sherlock," she says.

She is so utterly beautiful this close that his knees almost buckle.

"H . . . H . . . Hello."

"We shouldn't be fighting, you know. Mr. Hide is right. We should all be together."

"I agree," says Sherlock, before he can even think.

"Let us put the past behind us, what do you say?"

"I say that is wise."

"Walk with me."

She must have come alone, not a rare thing for this remarkable girl. She puts her arm through his and they move northward, up St. Martin's Lane, past the church. Irene Doyle has never been afraid to be seen in public with Sherlock Holmes. He has always appreciated that. Others stare after them, but she doesn't take notice.

They talk about politics. At least, she does. She despises Alfred Munby, but admires Disraeli, the Liberal Gladstone even more, and Bright and Hide the most. She believes that women should vote. Before they know it, they are on Montague Street, nearing her house.

"I am sorry for the way I have treated you," he says.

A pink glow comes to her cheeks.

"I understand."

"You do?"

"Well, I'm trying."

"Thank you."

"Would you like to come in?"

"I'm sure your father wouldn't –"

"He isn't home. He's out with Paul." There's a bitter tone in her voice.

"Then I shouldn't be inside. There would just be the two of us."

They had been alone in the house before, but that had been out of absolute necessity, when he was an escapee from jail, running for his life. It wouldn't be proper for him to be there now, not with a young lady of Irene's standing.

"Sherlock, this is a new day. If I want to have a gentleman in my home, I shall do so."

There is something in her expression that disturbs him. It isn't just her clothes that announce a new Irene. As he's walked with her today, he has been acutely aware of how completely she is changing – Miss Doyle is going to be a different sort of woman than he once imagined. She is becoming as bold and as expressive as her dress. In her conversation, he can feel her anger about life – about the time her father spends with her stepbrother, about women's roles, about not being allowed to state her true feelings, about being held down.

"Damn my father and brother," she says.

He gapes at her.

"Just being silly," she giggles. "Shocking word, isn't it?"

Sherlock goes in with her. They sit on the old settee where they used to lounge, and John Stuart Mill, her gassy little Corgi dog, waddles up to him and stretches out nearby. Holmes hopes the little mutt can keep his flatulence to himself.

Irene talks non-stop. It is as if she has been holding a flood of emotions back, and they are finally bursting forth. She says she loves little Paul, but that her father is soft in the head about him, attached to him as if Paul were the reincarnation of her dead brother.

"That's fine, if that's what he wants to do. It is time for me to cut the apron strings and be independent anyway. I am ready to be a new woman. He speaks of encouraging that sort of thing, but I doubt he wants me to be truly independent. I am sick of spending *all* my time helping him with his work. Not that I don't support him, but he is so removed from reality, even though he thinks he isn't. He doesn't really understand the unfortunate. He looks down on them from above and tries to get them to help themselves when that is often quite ridiculous. I would rather be truly close to them, understand them. Mr. Hide comes from a less-than-savory background. They say his father was a criminal, but he reformed. It makes him very authentic.

I want to be like that, somehow. I want to live a real life, connected to my feelings. I am learning a great deal from Malefactor. I think I am beginning to gain his trust."

Sherlock has to bite his tongue.

"Oh, I know you hate him. I know you think he wants to hurt you."

"He does, Irene."

"Not if you don't confront him." She slaps him playfully on the shoulder. "I have learned more about him. That's why I am sure I can change him. I know you know that his family pulled themselves up from nothing, and then lost everything. But did you know that he was a brilliant student too, a mathematical whiz who could have been a professor in any university?"

"It doesn't matter what he could have been. He chose otherwise."

"Yes he did, but he can turn back too. He could be such a positive force."

"I doubt it."

"I know you do. You have an old-fashioned view of someone's ability to change. He has spoken to me of his admiration for you, what do you think of that?"

"That he is using you."

She frowns. "You give me little credit, like most men do women. I am not naïve. I understand his evil tendencies, believe me. I shall alter him, bit by bit, before he harms you. And he is changing me."

Sherlock feels ill at ease.

"He has encouraged me to be myself, to not be the good little girl who simply accepts everything her father wants her to be."

"Is he encouraging you to commit crimes?"

"I shall ignore that comment. He is encouraging me to enjoy life, and to, among other things, explore my interest in singing. It connects me to my soul. You heard me sing, once."

"You are suited for better things."

"You sound like your grandparents."

"Pardon me?"

"Isn't that what they said to your mother? Didn't they try to hold her down? Didn't she love your father even though he wasn't deemed *suitable* for her? Didn't she give her life to their love, their marriage?"

He knows she is right.

"How well did I sing?"

"Uh . . ." he recalls her beautiful voice, her racy song, ". . . very well."

"I may actually take to the stage. I'm guessing that more than surprises you. But I want to do something different, and it is a worthwhile life, not disreputable as old-thinking snobs feel. The theater will be properly respected in the future – it not only addresses issues, explores true human emotions, it makes folks happy. Malefactor knows people who know people in the profession – powerful people. Perhaps I will go to America in a few years, create a whole new existence for myself, a whole new biography to put in the play programs and papers. Did you know that I had a wild American upbringing?"

She laughs, but Sherlock doesn't.

"I shan't marry someone my father chooses, either. I will marry whom *I* choose . . . or perhaps I won't marry at all! There is so much fun to be had."

Sherlock frowns.

"Oh, Master Holmes, you are so straightlaced! You need to bend a little. I am learning to, so can you. No matter what happens, I will still be me."

"I have a career path too, Irene. I think it not only worthwhile, but absolutely necessary. It is what I am destined to do."

"Then we both have our goals."

"You are under the influence of a blackguard."

"I am under the influence of myself, and a bad boy is not necessarily an evil one. Sometimes they are the most fun of all. But I tell you, Sherlock Holmes, I still know what is right and wrong. I will always help others, in my own way."

"Malefactor is fun?"

"Yes, fun. Shall I sing for you?"

"But the last time I heard you, you —"

"Didn't want to? I was shy about it, wasn't I? You will see I have changed. Just sit there and listen."

She stands up and tosses her hair. She begins to sing in that gorgeous voice he heard from the window at Christmas time last year. It is a love song, just as bold as the first one. She moves about in front of him, expressing the words with her actions. He feels uncomfortable, but also drawn in. The way she walks, lifts her arms, sticks out her hips, all makes him excited inside, though he tries to hide it. But when she lifts her dress to display her leg all the way up to her knee, he averts his gaze. She keeps smiling at him, looking right at him, making him look back, her face so happy it seems she will break down and laugh.

> I have a secret deep in my heart
> A little surprising
> And a little smart
> I enjoy a cigar
> I want to go far
> Ah, there's so much bliss
> In a stranger's kiss

Sherlock has sneaked into penny theaters before, heard comic belters sing rough songs, listened at the Royal Opera House to great voices with his mother . . . but he has never heard anyone sing like Irene Doyle. It isn't perfect, it isn't trained, but it conveys exactly what it intends.

And then she does it.

As she reaches the finish, she struts right up to him, places one of her heeled boots on the arm of the settee, leans down to him, bending like an acrobat . . . and kisses him . . . on the mouth. Her lips feel warm and a shock goes through him, starting in his chest and going down to his stomach. He knows he should pull away but he sits there and receives it. Only when she is done and smiling at him, does he jump to his feet.

"Irene!"

"I want to *live*, Sherlock. And I will."

11

Sherlock Holmes isn't the sort who looks forward to Friday as the best day of the week – he actually enjoys school, or at least he has for the past year. That is especially true the next day. The pressure from Beatrice and Sigerson Bell and in a sense, Lestrade to be involved with the Spring Heeled Jack case, vanishes when he reaches Snowfields. So do Malefactor and his threats, and for the most part, the irresistible attractions of Irene Doyle. It is such a relief. He can just relax and learn, knowing that his growth here is a key to his future. Only once or twice does he find himself thinking about Irene. He recalls that kiss. What she had said just before made a good deal of sense . . . in a way. Perhaps he is on the wrong path, is too stiff and narrow thinking. He has begun to wonder if he could, indeed, resume his friendship with her. She is becoming wayward. Perhaps she needs him. Perhaps they need each other?

By the end of the day, the headmaster is so pleased with Sherlock's work that he says he will clean and lock up on his own. He tells the boy he can go a little early. Holmes heads out, actually whistling a tune, unaware that it's the one he heard yesterday afternoon from the lips of Miss Irene Doyle.

His father, a scientist, taught him how to be an observing machine, and Sigerson Bell has taken the teaching even further. The old man likes to instruct him to be alert about everything at all times, including being attacked.

"You know the expression, my boy, have eyes in the back of your head? You, sir, if you are going to proceed with this future of yours, must have eyes everywhere: in the back of your legs, your spine, your hands, even peering out from your derriere! Learn to see, feel, hear, smell, and taste simultaneously and at all times. Be ever vigilant! It is a tenet of the Bellitsu practitioner!"

But Sherlock is so carefree after this happy school day that he leaves Snowfields, whistling that tune, without the least sense of vigilance. It is a decidedly unusual state for him, but he is enjoying it. He doesn't play any mental games as he strolls, doesn't try to exercise his brain. Instead, the powerful mind of Sherlock Holmes is startlingly blank.

And that, it turns out, isn't a good thing.

There are many alleys winding out from the little lanes near the school. Other than the railway station, Snowfields itself, a workhouse, and a few broken-down residences, this is an industrial area. Tradesmen are everywhere. They dump things in these alleys.

He doesn't notice the two smallish working-class men with their caps pulled down coming toward him until they have actually gripped him by both arms and lifted him into the air. In seconds, he is pinned against the wall at the back of an alley that takes a sharp turn after it leaves the street. He is out of view of pedestrians.

And the two hardworking "men" who are now slamming him against the wall . . . are in disguise. *Irregulars!* He looks up and sees Malefactor walking toward him with Crew and Grimsby on either side. The boss carries a big iron bar about four feet long. All three begin to remove their coats. Malefactor motions for the two who hold Holmes to leave.

"Stand by the entrance. Do not let anyone come in here."

He turns back to Holmes, looking angry, so angry that he is shaking.

"If you live through this beating, you will know how to conduct the rest of your life. And it shan't be as any sort of detective! If you do not live, I apologize to the fishes in the Thames for such a scrawny meal."

Grimsby lets out a cackle. His face is red and he is perspiring. He smiles like a lad about to enter a circus. He can barely contain his excitement. Beside him, Crew is impassive.

"I told you I would kill you, Sherlock Holmes. There will be little interest in a search for an insignificant half-breed like you. Lestrade will be happy to ignore it: your childish competition with Scotland Yard has given me *such* an opportunity. This . . . is a free kill!"

Sherlock can see he means it and is suddenly terrified. His stomach burns, his heart begins to race, and he feels as though he may be sick or soil himself. *This is how it is going to end for me. Child of a poor Jewish man . . . and a beautiful English lady, dead at age fourteen, nothing accomplished.*

"If you struggle, it will go worse with you."

"I will beat you with my fists, Jew-boy," growls Grimsby, "but if you calls out, I will smash your 'ead against that wall until your brains spill. The boss is going to break your legs and your arms and your ribs with that there railway bar. Take the blows that bust your bones and 'e may just leave you crippled . . . maybe!" He giggles again.

"What have I done? I'm not involved in anything!" cries Sherlock. He is almost weeping. "That report in the papers was –"

"I told you that chaos was good for me. The Greek myths, Christianity, even your Jewish lies, say the world began in utter chaos. That's our natural state. We should return to it. I admire the chaos theories in mathematics about numbers and equations spinning out of control. If you knew of them, you wouldn't. . . . You like order."

"I am doing nothing, now! I am refusing people who want me to help. I promise you!"

"He's afraid, Master, he's afraid!" Grimsby is jumping up and down, a vein protruding out on his forehead. Quivering, Holmes sets himself as best he can against the little villain, turning his hips toward him. But as he does, Crew comes up and grabs the boy's arms, wrenching them behind his back. Sherlock can smell the dye in his hair. He is a powerful boy indeed. Before Holmes can try to bring Crew down with a Bellitsu move, Grimsby has released a punch, aiming for the solar plexus, intending to start proceedings by rendering Sherlock helpless. Holmes has but an instant to tighten his abdomen.

"My boy!" cried Sigerson Bell just last week. "Should you ever be in the unenviable position of receiving a blow to the midsection, or a punch in the gut, as it were . . . you are out of luck!" The old man had laughed so hard that tears had come to his eyes. "Just playing the fool, Master Holmes, playing the fool. Now . . . strike me!"

And with that, he invited the boy to pound him in the abdomen. Sherlock tapped him lightly and the old man yelled at him to do it harder, whereupon Holmes added a slight bit of power to his blow, whereupon the apothecary cursed the boy with a truly revolting epithet – something to do with his ancestors resembling the refuse of a particularly repulsive beast – thus angering the lad so that he struck his old friend with everything he had . . . and discovered that he couldn't harm him. Sigerson Bell's gut, when engaged, was as hard as the pillars of St. Paul's Cathedral.

"Clench the abdominal muscles at precisely the right moment, my child! And actually step into the blow! It is an art in itself!"

Sherlock attempts to employ it as Grimsby delivers his punch, which arrives in a split second. His stomach muscles

are barely locked and hardened, and he has only begun to move toward the flying fist, but it is enough. Holmes doesn't buckle; he doesn't lose all the air in his body; he isn't left lying on the ground. Grimsby is astonished.

"Stand back!" commands Malefactor. Though the iron bar is heavy, he swings it as though it were a twig. Sherlock doesn't have time to be amazed at his enemy's strength. Digging in his heels, he shoves Crew back and is able to move him a few inches. The bar misses and connects with the wall, right in front of his thigh bone, making a dull clanging noise and chipping out a piece of stone.

Crew, pushed up against the wall by Holmes' maneuver, shoved so hard that most opponents would have buckled, doesn't flinch, doesn't utter a sound. His body feels as hard as the stone wall itself.

"Things are heating up in this city and that is good for my ventures," says Malefactor, pulling the bar from the wall. "Were I to allow you to have a healthy body and mind, you would soon not be able to resist being involved in chasing my Spring Heeled Jacks again! We have the Bobbies pre-occupied. But you would change that! After I warned you, you still kept interfering. You have proven to me that I must eliminate you. This is the perfect time to do it. You know too much about me, far too much! You are a thorn in my side, Sherlock Holmes, and if I do not stop you now . . . you will always be!" He glances at Crew. "Ready him!"

Crew swings Holmes around, cracking his head against the wall. The blinding pain shivers through his body right down to his toes. Crew swings him back and Malefactor lifts the iron bar to strike, to break his right thigh bone.

But the blow never comes. Someone clutches the weapon on the back swing.

The Spring Heeled Jack!

Its wings are widespread.

While both Grimsby and Crew gape at it, Malefactor turns and boots it in the midsection, knocking it across the alley and onto the ground.

"You are a fool!" cries the crime boss and advances toward it. It lies there gasping, one of its arms folded across its chest, as if wrapped in a sling inside its costume.

"Police!" it shouts. "POLICE!" That freezes the criminals. Malefactor motions and all three run.

"The next time, you will be dead!" Malefactor shouts at Sherlock.

The alley grows quiet. Only the sounds in the streets outside are heard, the distant buzz of Southwark.

"You 'ave a goose egg, you 'ave."

John Silver is sitting on the ground, half-dressed in his silly Spring Heeled Jack uniform, smiling up at Holmes. He is rubbing the arm that Sherlock broke, which is indeed wrapped in a sling under his crude costume.

"Thank you, Master Silver."

"Not at all. I is glad to be of service. I 'ave been thinking about a great many things lately, overhauling 'em, I 'ave, Master 'olmes, and I want to change the way I does things . . . just like you said. So I thought I'd start this afternoon. I lives east of 'ere in Rotherhithe. So I was a coming this way to start events off, to find Miss Beatrice coming home to the hatter's shop, to apologize to 'er. I was going to show 'er the costume to let 'er know 'ow ridiculous it was . . . and I am. Then I was going to throw it in a dustbin as she watched. The police didn't take it from me, you know, didn't bother. That Lestrade chap, 'e just smiled when Miss Beatrice and I told 'im about you and 'ow you 'elped 'er. I thought that peculiar. I 'ad told 'im what I did in order to raise you up a bit, because I felt wery guilty about things all of a sudden. You had been so brave and I such a fool, really. I 'ad got to thinking, straight off, when we was waitin' for the Peelers to come that night, 'ow awful I'd been to you over the years. I felt ashamed of everything, so I wanted to do something nice for you. I don't care if you is a Jew, Sherlock. Mr. Disraeli, 'e is one too. 'e is 'elping folks like me, I figure. 'e got the vote for me family. 'e is showing us all, 'e is. I don't imagine any of us is so different inside."

"No, I don't imagine we are."

"Well, I 'eard a commotion in 'ere, saw the two ragged boys at the entrance, 'eard that tall one with the tail coat and the top 'at shoutin' nasty things at you. So I slipped on me costume and came at them two little guards all of a sudden-like and they runs! Then I comes in 'ere. That tall one sure kicked me good. I 'ad it in mind to fight them. But I thought better of it when I felt 'is blow. And when I saw the looks of them two with 'im."

Silver rubs his stomach.

Moments later, as they leave the alley and head toward

Borough High Street, big John grabs Sherlock by the arm. He is looking back in the direction of Snowfields School.

"That's Beatrice, ain't it?"

Down Snowfields Road, way down near the school, Beatrice Leckie and her friend Louise are talking to the headmaster as he locks the door. The headmaster points toward Sherlock and Silver, or at least in their direction. They are so far away that the girls don't see them, but they begin to approach, eyes downcast, talking earnestly.

"She is a wery loverly one, she is," says Silver.

"Yes . . . she is."

"'ave you ever really conversed with her? I means, really sat down and 'ad a gab?"

"Well, we've chatted a little about –"

"You should. I did once, just once. It was when me guvna broke 'is back in an accident, building the new tracks out of London Bridge Station a few years past. Some rails fell off a wagon and landed on 'im."

"I didn't know that. I am sorry."

"Well, she 'eard, and she spoke to me. Sat right down and gabbed for the longest time. It was wonderful, it was."

Sherlock looks down the street at Beatrice. She still doesn't see them. She has pulled a piece of paper out of her pocket and is talking to Louise, waving it around as if frustrated about something.

"She gave me some money, she did."

"What? Her family can't spare any money."

"I knows. But she wouldn't 'ear of me family not 'avin it."

Beatrice looks up and spots Sherlock. Those black eyes glow.

"She is a political sort, you know."

"Nonsense. She doesn't know a thing about it. She is an old-fashioned girl."

"No, sir, she does. She says to me that day, she says that there should be money from the government for navies, workin' men like my papa who gets injuries, that no man in England should go without money if he is 'urt, none should starve either, even if they don't 'ave work. She says to me that things need to change in this country, and that the rich need to pay some of what they 'ave to 'elp the rest."

Beatrice waves.

"Did you know that 'er father is ill, that that's why she is working as a servant?"

"Sherlock?" cries Beatrice.

"Oh, my! I must go, Master 'olmes, I can't face 'er! She is just too loverly. I suppose that's why I wanted to scare 'er. I can't never face 'er without getting all me nerves up and shaking like a leaf, like I might just puke up me guts right there on 'er dress or something or –"

Silver runs. His long legs take him up the road and then into the crowd on Borough High Street. A short while later, Beatrice rushes up.

"Sherlock 'olmes, you are just the man I was searching for."

"Well, I am afraid you must make it brief, Miss Leckie. None of this Spring Heeled Jack stuff, I hope."

"You look disheveled, Sherlock. Your 'air is out of place." She smiles. "Not like you."

In all the excitement Holmes has done little about his clothes or his hair. That is indeed not like him. He straightens his old clothes, knocks off the dirt, and is about to fix his hair when he realizes that it is likely hanging down over the growing goose egg on his forehead. He doesn't want Beatrice to see it, so he resists perfecting his hair. It takes some doing.

"I suppose I was rushing home. Perhaps someone jostled me. Mr. Bell expects me not to dally after school, you know. I was then delayed by having the good fortune of meeting John Silver. He is really not such a –"

"Was that who that was?"

"Good fortune?" says Louise, curtsying to Sherlock as she begins. "'e was scaring us, 'e was, and an imposter to boot."

"You know, I have never had the pleasure of being acquainted with your surname, Miss Louise."

"It's Stevenson."

"Well, Miss Stevenson, I am well aware of what he was doing, but he is an earnest lad. Meant no harm, I'm sure. This silly Spring Heeled Jack scare has many folks acting strange."

"It ain't silly."

"I beg to disagree."

"It isn't silly, Sherlock," repeats Beatrice, dead serious. "I 'ave proof." She reaches into her dress and pulls out the piece of paper he had noticed in her hand minutes earlier. "The Spring 'eeled Jack was seen in three locations last night. The papers all 'ave it. And 'e fastened this . . . to our shop door."

She hands the note to Sherlock, but holds onto it as he reads. He notices that her hand is shaking. The note is written on the same paper that was left on Louise at Westminster Bridge.

I WILL KILL THE POOR, THE HELPLESS, THE FEMALES. JUST LIKE OUR GOVERNMENT. I'LL START WITH YOU! CHAOS!

The handwriting is similar to what was on the Westminster note too, and in the same blood-red color. Sherlock feels his heartbeat increase. Beatrice's hand is trembling so much that she lets go of the note.

"I took it from the door before father saw it, thank God. I 'aven't told the police . . . not yet. I thought I'd show it to you, that's 'ow much I trust you. Inspector Lestrade only 'as that one constable patrolling near us . . . and 'e's way out on Borough High Street."

Sherlock can see that she is trying hard to keep her composure and his heart goes out to her. She is being very brave.

"It isn't silly, Sherlock, it *really* isn't."

Holmes thinks for a moment. He returns the piece of paper.

"Don't . . . don't give this note to the police. It will only make things worse for you. Stay indoors tonight, with your entrance locked. I will see you tomorrow, bearing the means to protect you."

The boy considers how the Spring Heeled Jack struck in Knightsbridge at precisely the time he was pummeling John Silver in Southwark. *That fiend could not have been my old schoolmate.* He thinks of the reports of it appearing since then. He thinks of this note, written in the same hand as the first one, now threatening murder. He thinks of Malefactor, wanting him out of the way, right after the report appeared in *The Times* attaching his name to these sensations. He thinks of his enemy's use of the word *chaos*; he thinks of the fact that the Jack is threatening his close friend; he thinks of that friend, Beatrice, whom he has known since he was a child, since the days when their mothers were alive and well; Beatrice, so sweet and wonderful, threatened with murder, her soft, white hand shaking with fear; and finally he thinks of something Malefactor said, something the boy's fear had initially caused him to disregard. ". . . my Spring Heeled Jacks!" That's what Malefactor had said . . . "*my* Spring Heeled Jacks!"

Perhaps, thinks Sherlock Holmes, *a case has chosen me.*

12

The boy almost runs back to the shop. He doesn't even realize it. His mind is churning. Saturday and Sunday are before him, two days without school, two days to save Beatrice . . . and himself. He almost wonders if he should have taken her with him, installed her in the shop somewhere, safe with Sigerson Bell. But that would not only involve informing her father and terrifying him further – he must have been horrified that she was involved in the first attack – but would also make Beatrice less tantalizing bait. He hates to admit it, but he needs her to look like an easy victim, alone or with Louise, walking the streets in Southwark. He had been so careful to keep Irene out of danger, but now he is using Beatrice. He tries not to think of it.

He has three tasks before him. First, he must protect her. Then he must learn more about who Malefactor *really* is; where, other than roaming the streets, he might be found – best to know where your pursuer is at all times. And last, he must catch Malefactor or one of his gang in the act, hopefully about to commit murder, so that he is sent to prison for a long, long time. *But where can one find intimate facts about that secretive boy?*

"A pistol, my boy?" asks Sigerson Bell about an hour later.

"Yes, sir."

"I have one here, but I do not carry it. I consider it beneath my dignity to resort to such mechanical means of protection. And though I could procure another for you in an instant, I forbid you to carry one as well. You cannot have it."

"It is not for me."

"Not for you? And whom are you arming, sir?"

"Miss Beatrice Leckie."

Sherlock had wanted to keep the events of the day a secret, but he knows he can't, so he explains. First, he lifts his hair and displays his goose egg, now turning orange and purple. The apothecary lets out a cry and springs to his feet, rushing to his cabinet to retrieve a jar of frog eggs and another of lama milk, which he whips together with a mortar and pestle as Sherlock speaks, and applies to the boy's injury. But as Holmes gets to the part in his story where he receives this blow and explains what his enemy intends to do to him, the old man emits a shriek, his face turns an alarming shade of red, and he rushes up the spiral staircase.

"Sir?"

There is all sorts of noise coming from the floor above, pots and pans flying about, and a good deal of grunting and cursing from the old man. "Dog poop!" he exclaims. But then he is coming down the stairs, taking four at a time. He doesn't even look at Sherlock as he flies past. He has his own horsewhip in hand, is dressed in his bizarre fighting outfit, complete with obscene, tight leggings, a bandana tied around his head in combat mode, and his pistol tucked into his pants, right in the crotch.

Sherlock rushes after him.

"Sir? Sir, where are you going?"

They reach the front door.

"To eliminate a certain villain and his two lieutenants! This shan't take long! They shall not know what hit them!" He pulls the door open.

Sherlock slams it shut.

"Sir, you cannot do that. That would be murder!"

"And?"

"I don't think you would allow me to do such a thing."

"But . . . but . . . but they want to kill you, my boy. My own boy! I will stalk them until I find the three of them together. Then I will sneak up behind them, silent as a ghost! Then, I will employ the Bellitsu moves explicitly set out when one is confronted by three. I shall cartwheel and catch each, one after the other, with an upside-down kick to the jaw, rendering them all unconscious. Then, I will tie them up with my whip, explain to them, very calmly, what their crime is and how their lives must be terminated for the good of all . . . and then I'll shoot them!"

"No, you won't."

"I won't?"

"No, sir."

The old man's shoulders slouch. "No. No, I won't. It wouldn't be right, you are correct."

"You would be the villain and they the innocent victims."

"Hardly innocent."

"But before the law . . ."

"Yes, quite. We must catch them in the act!"

"We?"

"Well . . . you, Master Holmes, you . . . I suppose. And we must, indeed, arm Miss Beatrice!"

Bell is gone and back with a new pistol within the hour. It is an American model, a Smith & Wesson. "I know a cowboy," explains the apothecary, "helped him with his back . . . too much horse bucking, or whatever those people call it." He takes a few bullets out of his pocket, spins the chamber, loads the gun, and then fires a bull's-eye into the skull of one of his skeletons. Sherlock instinctively ducks.

"I will show you how to use this, and you will do the same for your young lady friend."

Sherlock had spent the time when Bell was gone writing a letter to Irene. In it, he asked for more information about Malefactor.

Bell's Apothecary Shop
Denmark Street,
London,

Friday March 6, 1868

Miss Doyle,

    It was lovely to spend some time with you yesterday. You indeed have a beautiful voice, and I agree that one must be oneself. And perhaps you are correct that we often aren't true to ourselves, deceive ourselves about what we want from life, present something false to the world, and are afraid to exploit our desires. It is an interesting idea.

    May I also say that I may be, as you say, misjudging Malefactor. Perhaps if I gave him the benefit of the doubt, approached him and spoke to him in a civilized manner, we might find common ground and get on better. Upon reflection, I know you are not naïve about him and that a little kindness and interest might, indeed, slowly help him change. I am intrigued to know more about him, and I thought I would ask you. Please write back and tell me more. What else has he told you about his past? I await both your response and seeing you again, some day soon.

        Warm regards,
        Sherlock Holmes Esq.

The letter goes into the post that night. He expects a response in the morning and he is not disappointed. There isn't a great deal that is new to him throughout most of her letter, mostly just tales of Malefactor's happy early Irish childhood, the family's downfall, his sister's death, his bitterness. Irene also writes that she can see through Sherlock's words, that he is trying to say nice things that he may not mean. At least, she says, he is trying. Then, right near the end, almost unknowingly it seems, she tells him something that rivets him – it is the opening for which he is looking.

> *Malefactor's followers are remarkably loyal. The only one I know of who has ever left him was an eccentric boy named Utterson, who took the money he made and went back to school. I've convinced Malefactor not to harm him, at least I hope I have. I believe the boy attends the Hermiston National School in Lambeth and is very conscientious, even goes there on Saturday mornings to clean up the rooms.*

Sherlock knows of the school. He tells Bell he is going out, tucks his horsewhip up his left sleeve, and makes for Lambeth as quickly as he can, sticking to the midst of the crowds and away from entrances to alleyways, constantly on the alert for Malefactor and the Irregulars. He reaches the Hermiston school safely, notices that the door isn't locked, and lets himself in. It is quiet inside the cool stone building, but from downstairs he can hear someone sweeping up on the first floor.

The former criminal has not lost his street-wise alertness, for by the time Sherlock Holmes enters the classroom, he has turned and is examining his visitor.

"Utterson?"

"Who asks?"

He is as eccentric as Irene said: as thin as a willow branch, dressed in a green jacket that looks like it is made of velvet, with light brown hair, so long that it almost touches his shoulders, flowing out from under a red and yellow skull cap. There is something of the artist, or at least Bohemian, in his appearance. *Sixteen years old, raised in Dublin, Ireland, sharp as a fox, a holder of secrets.* Sherlock presses his left arm to his side, making certain that his weapon is there.

"My name is Sherlock Holmes."

"And what do you want with me?"

"Why did he let you go?"

"I suppose there is no sense in pretending that I don't know to whom you are referring?"

"No."

"I know things, things I shan't tell you." He goes back to sweeping the floor.

"What if I made it worth your while to tell me?"

The boy stops sweeping. "And how would you do that?"

"I know I don't look like much, but I have been instrumental in helping the police capture several important criminals."

"I know."

Sherlock smiles. "I should have guessed."

"Your reputation precedes you in some quarters."

"Malefactor, Master Utterson, would be my greatest prize. And should he be removed to the luxurious quarters

of the Marshalsea Prison, you would never fear him again.
I am prepared to do whatever it takes to put him there."

"You assume I fear him now."

"Do you?"

"Not exactly, though I know you do."

Seldom does Holmes meet anyone who can size up
someone as quickly as he can. This boy is a contender.

"If you don't exactly fear him," continues Sherlock,
"then you are not entirely comfortable with his existence on
the streets of London, either."

The boy pauses and then motions toward the door.
"Walk with me as we talk. We must head downstairs. You
will be silent and I will speak. When we reach the entrance
you will act as if I sent you away. Our visit must be seen as
a very short one – a rejection. We will never meet again. He
is not who he says he is. He tells lies about his past. I knew
him when he was a child in Ireland. The family name is not
Malefactor – though it has its similarities. His father was
never a dustman. The family was well respected when I
knew of them, accepted in society, sending their children to
the best schools. Few were aware of their criminal activities,
though. Their wealth came from underground business
practices on the continent. They were found out by a gentleman who could benefit from their fall – he was about to
inform the police. They left Ireland before they were arrested,
and came to England. But their reign was over and they were
on the run. *That* is how his family fell, how they went to an
English almshouse where both his parents died – leaving him
with nothing but that tailcoat – and where his sister, the

only good soul in the family, died as well. He is bitter, yes, but because he believes that he and his family were singled out in a world where everyone is corrupt in some way, you and I, and the government too. We are all after power, he believes, especially the rich, and we all lie and cheat, but most of us pretend we don't. He considers himself an anarchist, saying the world would be better off in complete chaos, with each man for himself. He is a master debater on the subject. I am the only one who knows these things about his past, and I made sure before I left him that if anything happened to me, the police could trace my murder to him. I fear turning him in, but he fears killing me. We are at a stalemate. But you, Sherlock Holmes, can act. He lives in Knightsbridge by day – Queens Gardens off Brompton Road. He owns the white house there."

"He what?"

They are at the outside door. Utterson flings it open and shoves Sherlock into the street, so hard that he knocks him to the ground.

"And *stay* away from me!" he shouts. He strides up to Holmes and whispers into his ear. "I will get out of London when I am educated, change my name, go to the South Seas, and write adventure stories. Life, you see, is stranger than fiction, and my life has been unbelievable." He kicks Holmes in the ribs and storms away, slamming the school door behind him.

Sherlock rises slowly as people stop and stare. He doesn't know if he is more shocked by his sudden ejection and swift boot to the ribcage or by what Utterson has told him, especially what he said just before sending him flying out the door.

Malefactor lives in Knightsbridge?

He wants to go there immediately, but before he does, he must visit Beatrice. She will be home early on a Saturday, a half day for a scullery maid. It is nearing the noon hour. He walks east toward Southwark, the Smith & Wesson pistol deep in a pocket of his old frock coat.

The hatter, red-faced and looking unwell, is happy to see Sherlock Holmes and even happier to hear that the boy is calling on his daughter. She appears, beaming at him, almost the instant Sherlock's voice is heard at their front door. He steps inside, noticing today what he should have noticed before: how shabby the shop looks and that fewer hats hang from the hooks. There are no customers to be seen. Beatrice wraps a thick woolen shawl around her shoulders, and as they step out together into the brisk March air, she puts her arm in his.

"I am told you are a political thinker, Miss Leckie."

She colors. "Who told you that?"

"A little birdie, actually a big, silver one."

"Oh, Master Silver! 'e thinks that anyone with an opinion is a deep thinker. I suppose 'e remembers my chat with 'im. I was angry about 'is father's situation, that's all. I leave politics up to the competent men of this nation . . . leaders like Mr. Disraeli."

They stop down the street and he edges her into an alley.

"Sherlock?"

"I have something for you."

"You do?"

He pulls the pistol from his pocket and she gasps.

"What is that for?"

"For you."

"Me? But I don't know 'ow to use it."

"I will show you. I want you to be safe. Carry it with you at all times. If the Jack attacks you, do not hesitate to point it at him. That will likely be enough, but use it if you must. It will be self-defense. And by the way . . . I am now certain who this villain is."

"You are? But who —"

"Never mind, that's not your concern. I'll tend to accosting him, just carry this and keep yourself safe. That way, you won't need the police around your door, upsetting your father."

"Yes, Sherlock."

He shows her how to load it, point it, and fire, though she can't practice here in the alley. Strangely, she doesn't seem to take it seriously. She appears more interested in having him show her, than in really learning. She keeps getting him to stand near her and wrap his hand around hers as she holds the gun. She doesn't ask any questions about the Spring Heeled Jack. She doesn't even seem to fear him. It appears she would rather just be close to Sherlock.

She is a brave girl . . . but if she only knew who this villain is . . .

It is a good hour's walk to Knightsbridge. Clouds gather in the cool day as he finds his way eastward through Lambeth and crosses the Thames at Westminster Bridge. It has been a full week since Beatrice and Louise were attacked here. He stands on the south side of the bridge near Astley's Theatre and looks across the wide, brown river with its crowd of noisy boats of all sizes, and up at the Palace of Westminster with Big Ben rising above it. He imagines the Spring Heeled Jack perched on the balustrade wall, the government buildings framing him. Now that he considers things, with more facts in hand, this whole sensation is exactly Malefactor's style. He put the fear of God into those dear girls, but made sure they survived to tell their tale. He saw to it that one of them was Sherlock's friend. *Malefactor knew it would draw me in, force me to protect Beatrice, and do it on my own, which would put me out on dangerous streets at night and make me vulnerable to a deadly attack.* Malefactor could eliminate the thorn in his side and have the deed done by a disguised perpetrator who would frighten all of London and bring chaos to the city when fear and uncertainty was at its height. He started proceedings on Westminster Bridge, with the symbol of the Empire's stability as audience. He figured low-lifes would try to imitate the Jack, and things would begin to spiral. It was, and is, a deep and tangled plan, accomplishing many things in just a few bounds. His opponent, Sherlock must admit, is a genius.

He passes Westminster Abbey and moves up Birdcage Walk past the big green expanse of St. James's Park, the queen's massive urban lawn with her swans on its ponds, fronting Buckingham Palace. Even the strolling pedestrians look nervous today. Governesses with children, young men with young ladies, nannies out with babies in prams – all seem to be glancing around. There is a fiend on the loose. The city is uneasy. *Or is it my imagination?* He crosses in front of the palace, serene and majestic as usual, and goes up Constitution Hill toward Knightsbridge Road. *Can Malefactor really live in this wealthy neighborhood?* A different fear crosses his mind. Is this a setup? *Irene is Malefactor's friend now. Did she intentionally tell me about that boy, Utterson . . . or whatever his name really is? Can Irene be trusted anymore? Are Utterson's directions leading me into some sort of dead-end in a Knightsbridge neighborhood where I will be mugged and beaten by the Irregulars?* He warily watches for little figures darting at him from either side. But something comforts him, at least somewhat: this isn't Malefactor's time of day. He's noticed that the crime boss rarely does much when the sun is out.

At Hyde Park Corner, where rich Belgravia and Mayfair meet, he goes through the Wellington Arch with its ridiculously large statue of the late Duke of Wellington atop, aboard his famous charger, Copenhagen. Wellington's old home is nearby, known to citizens as "Number One, London." The great national hero, the vanquisher of the legendary Napoleon, should be here now, calming things. *Or should he?* Sherlock remembers that when the Iron Duke was prime minister, he always opposed reform, and even had unbreakable bars installed on his windows to protect him from the mobs who sought changes.

The boy walks along Knightsbridge on the south side of Hyde Park and turns down Brompton Road. No worries here – many wealthy folks, the poor who supply them and work for them, and a few vendors who pursue them, make up a flow of pedestrians on the wide foot pavements – not a place for an attack.

He passes a little store named Harrods, selling groceries and other goods and spots Queens Gardens. All the streets going off from Brompton Road have been wide ones, lined with big, elegant homes. Queens Gardens is narrow. His fears return. *Should I go down here? Can Malefactor really live here?* It seems preposterous.

He turns around and walks back up Brompton Road, then crosses it through the gleaming carriages and well-groomed horses, to Lancelot Place on the other side, and begins to pace, trying not to look conspicuous, unsure what to do. A few gentlemen stare as he goes by, but he keeps his eyes down.

Coming here is against his best instincts. He doesn't have many facts, just a story that a boy told him, a boy whose identity and past is not certain. And finding Malefactor here – the gang leader who he thought lived on the streets and who he knows sleeps there at times – is growing increasingly improbable as he sees more and more impressive homes. But Sherlock has to save himself and Beatrice. Irene may not be who he thought she was, but he doubts she would purposely harm him. He has to take a chance. He lets his horsewhip drop down in his sleeve, the handle falling into the palm of his left hand, then saunters down Brompton Road again and enters Queens Gardens.

The street actually widens as he walks, opening up into a beautiful avenue lined with big trees. The houses are not quite as large as those in most of Knightsbridge, but they are certainly respectable. And there, right at the end, almost tucked away in the trees . . . is a modest white one, just as Utterson said. There are a few people walking along the foot pavement in this cul-de-sac. He acts as though he has a reason to be there. *It is in your walk.* He remembers his mother's advice about acting. *Take on a character.*

Sherlock approaches the house at a brisk pace, a hand in his pocket as if he is a messenger boy with a note to deliver. But the home looks empty. All the shutters, even those on the door, all as white as the stone exterior, are closed. Sherlock certainly can't knock at the entrance. He is at the end of the street, right in front of the house. He glances around. No one is looking his way. He can only hope that a resident isn't peering out a window at him. He slips up close to the building and darts into a tall row of shrubs and gets himself behind them, completely obscured from view.

He waits a long while. A nearby church bell chimes two separate times. He slouches down onto the cold ground.

At least two hours later, the shutters begin opening so quietly that Sherlock, almost asleep despite the cool day, barely hears them. Then, the front door opens. He peeks carefully around the shrubbery. A man, medium height and well-dressed in a dark suit with black bowler hat and white cravat, is coming out. He locks the door, tries it, locks it a second time, and tries it again. He turns and eyes the street, glances both ways, up and down. He surveys the front of the house. Sherlock ducks low. Then the man heads out along the street, whistling, poking his cane into the foot pavement with each sprightly step. He wears thick glasses and has a big black beard.

Holmes considers entering the house. But that quickly seems like a disastrous idea. If this really is Malefactor's home, Sherlock can't be caught in there. But who was that man? *Is he an associate? A relative? Is Malefactor's father still alive?*

There is only one option that makes sense: follow him.

Sherlock checks that no one is looking his way and leaves the shrubbery as quickly as he can. He's on the foot pavement in a flash and heading down the street. In the distance, he sees the man turn right, onto Brompton Road, heading for the center of London, back the way Sherlock came.

But at the bottom of Constitution Hill, by Buckingham Palace, he doesn't head for Birdcage Walk and Westminster Bridge. Instead, he strolls on the tree-lined pedestrian avenue on the north side of St. James's Park and moves toward the bustle of the city via Trafalgar Square. Sherlock wonders if he is a businessman of some sort. If so, what business would a co-resident of Malefactor's conduct?

There aren't as many newspapers on Saturdays but the square is just as busy, since foreigners and folks from the country with a little money come to the city to see the sights when the week is over.

Sherlock spots Dupin selling his publications. "A Double Jack Attack!" he cries. The boy left the apothecary's shop before their papers arrived. He wishes he could read that story. *Two more attacks? Where? When? Was anyone hurt?* But he can't pause here. He must stay on the trail.

Once they get past the square, the bearded man's pace picks up. They enter The Strand, lined with hotels and famous West End theaters. He passes The Adelphi, where comedy rules, then Exeter Hall, one of the great political gathering places in the Empire. Though a stranger looking at its small entrance between two Corinthian pillars would never suspect as much, John Bright has many times riveted audiences within its walls, and may soon need to again. As the bearded man passes the magnificent Lyceum Theatre, that seems to glow even when unlit, he looks behind him. Sherlock has kept well back, hidden in the crowd. *Why is the fellow looking back?* He is also pulling an empty sack of some sort from a pocket. He darts up the street, crosses it quickly – almost into an oncoming horse – and disappears into a lane going east. This part of London is full of such lanes and alleys, running like spiderwebs from the more familiar thorough-fares. Sherlock loses sight of the man and frantically tries to cross the street. But it takes a while, and when he gets to the lane's entrance there is no sign of the gentleman. Then, far ahead, he spots him coming out of an alley . . . wearing a different coat! Sherlock runs to get closer and as he nears, notices that the man looks slimmer . . . and that the coat is a worn tailcoat. The sack is bulging.

The man stops for an instant and leans over and puts his hand to his face as if rubbing his eyes. When he raises his head, Sherlock can just see the side of his face well enough to tell that he has removed his glasses. They come to Drury Lane and cross it near the theater. The man slips down another alley. When he emerges this time . . . he is beardless! That's when Sherlock recognizes his walking stick.

Malefactor!

It seems that the young mastermind indeed lives in Knightsbridge, probably alone, funded by the huge take from his thriving criminal business. He disguises himself until he nears his gang. As always with this rascal, he has created a brilliant situation: he is permanently in hiding in a very unlikely place; he doesn't run the risks that his followers do, stays healthy and warm and always elusive. If that boy can manage all this at such a young age, what will he accomplish when he becomes an adult?

In minutes, Malefactor, still hatless, is at Lincoln's Inn Fields. It is the largest park in the city and a daily haunt for his Irregulars, a perfect place for them to be inconspicuous. Sherlock stops a distance away, sees Malefactor enter the park and head toward the far end, to a well-treed area. Grimsby appears and tosses him his top hat.

An idea comes to Sherlock. *I must get closer.* Turning on his heels, he runs back through the crowds, down Drury Lane, along The Strand and into Trafalgar Square.

"Mr. Dupin!" he cries.

The old newsboy looks up at him from his kiosk and smiles.

"Funny, Master 'olmes, how this 'ere Spring 'eeled Jack situation come up right after you talks to me about 'im."

"I have a request."

"More information?"

"No, your clothes."

"I beg your pardon?"

"I want your hat and your coat."

"Naturally. I suppose you won't be telling me why?"

"No, sir."

"Just your average request, asking for the coat off a man's back."

"And your hat."

"Of course, me 'at too."

"I'll . . . I'll give you a sixpence."

"No, you won't. If it were anyone but you, 'olmes, I'd say no, but I'm inclined to comply. Especially if you –"

"Explain all about it when it's over?"

"You've got it, mate."

"Done. Here's my coat." Sherlock removes his old frock coat in a flash. "Sorry, I don't have a hat."

The poor cripple, well-muscled through the chest and arms from years of propelling his cart, deftly pulls off his coat and hands over his hat. Getting Sherlock's frock coat on is a more difficult task. It is so tight that it looks like a straightjacket.

"I can't look like this long, 'olmes, it will affect me reputation."

"I'll be back in a bit."

Sherlock rushes off. The big brown coat, thick and woolen to protect against the wind, smells of tobacco, but with its collar up and the soft felt cap pulled down over his eyes, Holmes is unrecognizable. He is back at Lincoln's Inn Fields in minutes. He slows his breathing and walks past the Irregulars several times. They are on the other side of the black wrought-iron gate that surrounds the park. Sherlock screws up his mouth, his only visible part, to complete the disguise.

Despite several passes he can't hear much of what they are saying. They keep their voices muted. But on his final pass, worried that he has left Dupin too long with his thin, tight coat, he hears five words from Grimsby, just as Malefactor takes his leave from the gang.

"Dusk tonight, then? Right 'ere."

It is enough.

13

It is now well into the afternoon and Sherlock hasn't done a single one of his chores at the shop, and yet he still has something to accomplish before he goes home. He races to Trafalgar Square, exchanges clothes with Dupin, asks him for a piece of paper, writes a note, folds it, addresses it to G. Lestrade, and rushes off to Scotland Yard. Careful not to be seen by the senior inspector, he leaves the message with the desk sergeant and sprints back to Denmark Street.

He is certain that Malefactor is heading home. But catching him in his residence does nothing, for he isn't, on the surface, guilty of anything. He, or one of his followers, must actually be caught as the Spring Heeled Jack.

Sherlock has a plan.

He is certain that the shutters on the white house at Queens Gardens stay closed whenever Malefactor is at home and are open when he is out. He wants the young boss to be with his followers when one of them, likely Crew, turns into the Jack – Sherlock must be sure that his prime target goes to work this evening. All he has to do is get to Queens

Gardens tonight and see if the shutters are closed, indicating that Malefactor is at home. He will follow him when he emerges, young Lestrade (armed with a revolver) by his side. They will watch the Jack come to life, and then, if they are smart about things, watch it attack someone. They should be able to take Malefactor and his villains at gunpoint before they really hurt anyone. He can give the credit to Master Lestrade, supply him with information about the other crimes the Irregulars have committed, and see if Scotland Yard can find a way to send the gang and their leader to jail and throw away the key.

At the apothecary's, Sherlock reads the newspaper reports of the Spring Heeled Jack's latest exploits. Though the article is on the front page and features a large, black headline, there is little in last night's appearances – two of them, in opposite ends of the city, about an hour apart – that tells him much. The fiend got away easily each time and the descriptions of him, given by the working-class women whom he attacked, were sensational and difficult to accept as the truth – blue flames coming from his mouth, red eyes and devil-ears, and two wildly different descriptions of a bizarre, angry face, hissing the word *chaos*! The only information of note comes from the second attack. During it, the villain seemed intent upon truly hurting its victim, beginning to physically assault the unconscious girl. Fortunately, it was interrupted by two burly tradesmen who happened to be walking by after a late night at a public house. It seems as though the Spring Heeled Jack is turning more violent, and that if he can get at someone and not be interrupted . . . murder may, indeed, be the result.

Sherlock gives himself a good head start, leaving almost two hours before dusk. He tells Bell that he is planning to meet Beatrice in Southwark, which the old man approves of, given the increasing aggressiveness of the Jack. It doesn't take the boy long to get to Knightsbridge – it is almost directly east of where he lives. Not confident in Master Lestrade's ability as a snoop, he has asked the boy to meet him at the Wellington Arch and keep out of sight. It is perfect because there is a tiny police station built right into the arch, which a single constable occupies, and where the inspector's son can hide. Sherlock will then go to Queens Gardens, trail Malefactor, and pick up Lestrade on the way back, hopefully as their suspect walks to Lincoln's Inn Fields.

But when Sherlock arrives, young Lestrade isn't there. An hour later, he still hasn't come and Holmes turns restless. *Did someone intercept my note at Scotland Yard? Perhaps Master Lestrade doesn't want to work with me, or couldn't obtain a revolver.* He keeps circling the roundabout where the arch sits, staying out of the constable's sight. *Should I do this on my own? Should I go to Queens Gardens now?* All he has is his horsewhip, a poor weapon against a gathering of Irregulars. But he will have make do. It is time to move. He will go alone, whether ill-advised or not.

Just as he is leaving, he hears a voice.

"Sherlock!"

Master Lestrade is puffing as he runs through strolling tourists toward the arch. He is wearing his checked brown suit and bowler hat, a thick woolen comforter thrown around his neck against the cool March evening. Something bulges in his pocket.

"My apologies."

"That may not do. He may be gone."

"My father didn't leave the office until very late. I couldn't take the pistol until he left the building. I have it here. I stole it from his desk."

He offers an uneasy smile and then begins to pull it from his pocket. Sherlock grips his hand.

"Not here!"

"Oh, yes, of course."

Holmes doesn't like what he sees: Lestrade is sweating, and he speaks in quick bursts. That's not simply because he has been running. He is nervous. The attempt to pull a police revolver from his pocket in plain view at busy Hyde Park Corner announces that loud and clear. Sherlock needs a competent ally tonight. Otherwise, he might very well end up dead.

"Calm yourself."

"I . . . I am ready to fight evil, to collar the villains who have attacked Miss Leckie. I am as serene as the Lake District."

"Are you?"

"Look to yourself, Sherlock Holmes. I have been trained by the best."

The boy wants to say that is what worries him, but he bites his tongue.

"Your tardiness may have destroyed our opportunity. I will hurry to Queens Gardens. Hopefully, Malefactor has not left yet, and I will not be observed. That would be catastrophic. Wait here and stay out of sight. If all goes well, I will pick you up on the way by."

Sherlock turns to whisk along Knightsbridge Road, but stops in his tracks.

"Behind the arch! Now!"

"But why? . . . I don't see –"

Sherlock snatches Lestrade by the collar and pulls him behind the hulking stone arch.

"He's coming!"

"I can't see –"

"He is in disguise, wearing a bowler, glasses, and black beard. I shall tell you when it is time to move."

Sherlock waits a good minute before he peeks out from behind the gray stones. Sure enough, Malefactor has passed by and is heading down Constitution Hill, exactly like he did this afternoon. The sun is beginning to set.

"We shall keep a good distance. I am guessing he will take the same route."

And so he does. Sherlock stays well back, much farther than when he followed his rival earlier in the day, so concerned is he about Lestrade's abilities. The older boy continues to be nervous, holding one arm carefully over the pocket containing the pistol, eyes riveted ahead, obviously in pursuit of someone. Sherlock has to keep reminding him to look nonchalant.

Malefactor begins to discard his disguise once he gets to the other side of Trafalgar Square and into the smaller streets, just as he did before. Lestrade is amazed. But Sherlock makes sure that his detective friend doesn't get too close a look. In fact, once they have reached Lincoln's Inn Field, he won't let the other boy enter the park or stand anywhere near the wrought-iron fence. He wants him somewhere on the far side of the street that surrounds the rectangular field.

The College of Surgeons is at the south end of the park, a big gray building with six Corinthian columns at its regal entrance and a black fence surrounding it. Sherlock knows this place well because Sigerson Bell always talks about it – its basement contains an amazing collection of scientific artifacts and bizarre oddities. The boy has sat in the park many times and stared at the building, imagining its innards. He's also noticed two things about its exterior: there is a tight walkway between it and another building, about as wide as a man's shoulders, and a gas lamp almost directly in front on the street. This will be a perfect place for Lestrade to wait, hidden and out of the way, and yet able to see the park. Sherlock is guessing that Malefactor will send his Spring Heeled Jack south of the river tonight, since many attacks have occurred there in working-class areas, and that is where Beatrice lives. The best way to get out of the Lincoln's Inn Field area and go southward would be to leave the park by the entrance directly in front of the College.

It is a residential area, and only a few people are about at this darkening hour. Sherlock deposits his complaining partner in the walkway by the College, just out of view, telling him to remain silent and still. Lestrade is only to move when Sherlock appears and gives him a signal. Even then, he is to follow behind.

The Irregulars are convening at the opposite side of the field, under a cluster of big trees that provide cover. Sherlock doesn't dare get close. Instead, he takes a long route around the park and stops at the north-east corner, well out of sight and a good fifty feet away. Still, he is able to look through the bars of the black iron fence and at least make out the outlines of the Irregulars in the growing darkness.

Two gang members are posted as lookouts in the park at a distance from each other and eight more are gathered in a circle around someone. The one in the middle is not Malefactor. Sherlock can see the boss's tall top hat in the ring of boys looking on. There are eleven visible gang members in the eerie light. *There should be twelve Irregulars plus Malefactor, for a total of thirteen. Where are the other two?* This makes Holmes nervous. He glances around; he looks back. The shadowy boys are making their circle tighter, closing ranks, so it is difficult to see exactly what the one in the middle is doing. But Sherlock *can* see that he is tall . . . and that he appears to be pulling on something that looks like black wings.

Time to leave and rush back to Lestrade – they are about to unleash the Jack!

Sherlock moves slowly at first, trying not to make a sound, but when he is farther away, runs, ignoring the looks he gets from three gentlemen who walk past. He is glancing around, wary of a sudden attack by the two absent Irregulars.

His breathing is getting heavier, sounding awfully loud in the quiet park area, but not so loud that as he turns the corner and heads up the street toward the College of Surgeons, he doesn't hear the sound of a few voices . . . and someone moaning.

He looks up and sees something hanging from the lamppost in front of the College, a dark lump in the circle of soft light.

"They put him up there so fast I couldn't even help him. There was two of them, two lads."

"You saw it?"

"Is he dead?"

"Not by the way he's moanin'."

Master Lestrade is hanging from the lamppost, upside down like a bat, tied to it by his long woolen comforter, watched by two respectable-looking men and a couple, the woman averting her eyes.

Sherlock sprints to the post and shinnies up.

"What are you doing lad? That's not how we should proceed. I'll call the police."

"Someone should look into this."

Sherlock doesn't want that. It will end his investigation, to say nothing of the deep embarrassment and harm it will cause young Lestrade's career in the Force. In a minute, Holmes has unknotted the comforter and allowed Lestrade to slide down the post. The older boy crumples on the foot pavement, still groaning. Sherlock undoes the other end of the comforter from his feet and slaps him across the face.

"Get up!"

"I think you should let him be, lad."

"Police!"

Sherlock pulls Lestrade up onto his pins. The young detective's eyes are opening and becoming clear.

"Master Holmes! They attacked me so fast I didn't get to pull out my –" He reaches for his revolver. "It's gone!"

Sherlock's heart sinks. They've armed the Irregulars with a police revolver. But that is the least of his concerns now.

"Can you run?"

Though Lestrade has taken a blow to the head, Sherlock knows that, despite his inadequacies, the other boy has a deep inner resolve.

"I am as fit as a fiddle!" he says, swiping his bowler hat off the ground and clapping it onto his head. He follows when Holmes starts to run, away from the park and through the narrow roads toward the river.

"Lads! Come back!" one of the spectators calls.

Both boys have the same idea. *Go south. Seek Beatrice. She is in trouble.*

They get across Blackfriars Bridge in no time, running with everything they have. Once into Southwark, they turn east and head through the smaller lanes, Sherlock leading them along shortcuts. He has no fear tonight – together, these two can fend for themselves – though he wonders what they will do if they encounter the Spring Heeled Jack near the hatter's shop. Now they have only the horsewhip and their bare hands. Their enemies have the gun, but that doesn't matter now. They must arrive before the fiend can.

Halfway between Blackfriars Road and Sherlock's old neighborhood, just past the Barclay and Perkins Brewery, out of breath, they stop momentarily where the London Bridge and Charing Cross Railway Line runs above a street. The boys bend over, hands on their knees, chests heaving. There's no one on the street but Sherlock Holmes and Master G. Lestrade.

Or so they think.

Holmes is the first to hear the noise – a heavy breathing and low growl above them. He looks up to see a man dressed as a bat, scurrying along the tracks, its wings fluttering in the air. At least he thinks it is man. In some ways, it's more like an animal.

"Oh!" exclaims Lestrade.

It sees them. For an instant it pauses on the edge of the bridge, looking down, ready to jump. It lets out a full-throated growl. They can see its face, fairly bursting with anger. Its black hair is matted and greasy, something like horns stick out from its scalp, red eyes bulge, a vein stands out on its forehead, and while it perches rather like a vulture, it lets out a cry. "Chaos!" it shrieks, and a blue flame comes from its mouth. It wears huge black boots.

Is this the REAL Jack? Can it be Crew? thinks Sherlock. Fear surges through his veins. He feels sick to his stomach. Were it to attack him now, he wouldn't be able to move. But it jumps from the tracks onto a nearby building, a long dangerous leap of nearly ten feet, and vanishes into the night.

For a few moments there is silence.

"What, in the name of God, was that?" Lestrade's voice is quavering.

"I don't know. But it came from direction of the hatter's shop."

14

A HARROWING ATTACK

They fly toward the shop, but it seems as if they are too late. A little crowd is gathered up a lane just past the hatter's door. They are looking down at someone, crumpled on the cobblestones. It is a girl. Sherlock recognizes Beatrice's red bonnet lying nearby.

He beats Lestrade to the spot and bursts through the little group, pushing people aside. "Beatrice!"

She lifts her head. Sherlock sighs in relief and Lestrade comes forward. But her face looks ashen, tears roll down her cheeks, and an angry welt is evident on her forehead. Holmes leans over her. The instant he does, she puts her arm around his shoulder and pulls him close. Her lips are right to his ear.

"You've come. I knew you would. I tried to use the pistol, Sherlock, I truly did. But I was too frightened, and he was on me too fast. I just stepped from the door to throw out the wash water and he leapt at me. He took the gun."

"Clear off!" Lestrade addresses the crowd, puffing out his chest. "I am with the London Metropolitan Police."

"You is?" asks someone.

"You're just a lad!"

"He *is* with the police!" says Beatrice, struggling to her feet with Sherlock's help. "Call the Force, Master Lestrade. They must come immediately. Do you have a whistle? There's supposed to be a constable patrolling out on Borough 'igh Street."

"You," says Lestrade, full of confidence now as he extends a finger at a burly man, "head out and put up a cry for the Bobbies. There should be more than one close by."

Sherlock doesn't want that. "Before you go," he says, stopping the man, "did anyone see this happen?"

"Who are you? Are you a policeman too? Is this the children's brigade?"

The crowd laughs.

"Did anyone see this happen?" snarls Sherlock.

"I didn't, not me," says a woman in a dirty brown bonnet.

"Not I," says a boy, not much older than Sherlock. "I runs out 'ere cause I 'ears the Leckie girl screaming terrible. I just sees her lying on the ground 'ere."

The burly man sets out, bellowing. "Police!" The rest begin to disperse.

"Take me in," says Beatrice in a weak voice. "Father will be home soon. I don't want him to see me like this."

Lestrade rushes over and takes an arm, while Sherlock grips her by the other. They support her, gently walking her into the hatter's shop. Holmes knows he can't stay. He doesn't want to be here when the police arrive. Inspector

Lestrade is looking for a reason to shame him, perhaps even to find a charge against him.

"Master Lestrade," says Beatrice as she is set down on a chair, "you must tell your father that you saw this with your own eyes."

"I will, Miss Leckie, I most certainly will. We must put the full might of the police against this fiend now." He takes his hat off and glows at her.

"So," asks Sherlock, "you were alone when this happened?"

"I think so."

Trust no one. She was completely alone? Holmes has questions about the attack, but when Beatrice drops her head down to her chest in exhaustion, any sense of suspicion vanishes. There is blood oozing from wounds on her neck.

"Miss Leckie!" cries Lestrade.

"Is it bad?" she asks.

"Master Lestrade, you must tend to her. There are clean clothes in the back room where the family lives and a pump out front in the little square. Put some water on those lacerations. And have her come to see Mr. Bell tomorrow. He works wonders with infections."

"I am quite capable of looking after her. And *I* shall find her a *real* doctor tomorrow."

"I must go."

Sherlock heads for the door and Lestrade removes to the back room. But just as Holmes is going out, Beatrice speaks to him in an anguished voice. "I have another injury, I think, on my leg. It's . . . up high."

Sherlock turns. She is lifting her dress . . . and the undergarments. He sees her smooth white skin above her ankle, and then his eyes go up her shapely calf, past her knee, and the curve of her thigh. Up there, he sees another welt.

"I . . . I . . . yes," says Sherlock.

"Have you ever seen such a thing?"

"No. No, Beatrice, I haven't."

She lowers her dress and weakly smiles at him.

"I must be off!" He stumbles out the door.

But he doesn't go far. He waits in the shadows until the police come, two Peelers on the run. He expects Lestrade to emerge soon, but he doesn't. It must be half an hour later, after the hatter has returned and more police arrive, that young Lestrade finally appears at the door.

Sherlock pounces on him as he walks past.

"OH!" he cries, his voice an octave higher than usual.

"Calm yourself, Romeo."

"I . . . I am as calm as –"

"The Lake District?"

"You have no cause to call me Romeo!"

"I don't?"

"No, you don't. And if you persist . . . I will box your ears."

"Or shoot me with your pistol while hanging upside down from a lamppost?"

"Don't tell my father."

"Of course not . . . if you do me a favor in return. Stop by Scotland Yard on your way home and tell me if there is any news of Spring Heeled Jack attacks over the last few hours. And if so, I'd like some details, something the papers won't have. We can walk there together. I'll wait for you down White Hall Street."

"I don't need to."

"I beg your pardon?"

"The last few Bobbies who responded to our call were chattering like monkeys. They said they heard there were as many as three attacks tonight. The city will be terrified."

"Three attacks?"

"And one wasn't like the others."

"What do you mean?"

"There was murder tonight, Sherlock."

"Murder?"

"You won't believe what he's done."

15

A HALL OF MIRRORS

Sherlock finds it difficult to get to sleep that night. Master Lestrade hadn't been able to give him many details. What the young detective knew was that the Bobbies were certain that the Spring Heeled Jack had committed murder of a most gruesome kind, that the policemen who were on the scene came back with blood covering their boots, as if they had been wading through it. The Bobbies said there were rumors swirling in the city about it and that they couldn't say more. They'd been told that policemen were being pulled from their beds and posted throughout London, and their Commissioner was talking about putting a Bobbie "on every street corner."

As Sherlock tries to settle down in his wardrobe bed, his mind is racing, imagining the events of last night and who the Jack really is. All he knows for certain is that Malefactor must have had a hand in at least one of the attacks, and that his rival isn't above committing murder. *How far did he go?*

Holmes tries to distract himself by reading a short story by Edgar Allan Poe. Perhaps a fictional nightmare can replace a real one. But it doesn't work. He sets it aside and lies back, listening to Bell tossing and turning upstairs, and as he finally starts to fade to sleep, he thinks the old man has risen and is descending the spiral staircase, dressed as the Spring Heeled Jack. But when he awakes with a start all is silent.

He puts his head back on his feather pillow and is suddenly out in the city at night, crossing Westminster Bridge, rats scurrying along the cobblestones, crows cawing on the House of Commons, and bats swarming in the black sky above. As he glances up to them, he sees the Jack on the balustrade wall and then notices Beatrice and Louise running at the other end of the bridge. The Jack rises and leaps after them at supernatural speed, closing in with each gigantic bound.

Sherlock tries to run after them, but his feet are glued to the ground. He looks down and sees he is stuck in congealed blood. He has the sense that he is being observed. He turns and sees another Jack perched on the balustrade! It has Crew's face. Sherlock hears a hiss and turns to the opposite side of the bridge. Another Jack is perched there! It has Sigerson Bell's eyes. Another is near it, looking like Munby, a fourth is Malefactor, another John Silver, a sixth Irene, and another . . . Louise.

Holmes looks down the balustrades and sees that they are filled with Spring Heeled fiends, all the way to Southwark. And across the river he spots them flying from the buildings, huge dark bats in the sky. He turns back to the House of Commons: the Jacks are lining it and the House of Lords, and a cluster is roosting on Big Ben. A veritable swarm upon the Palace of Westminster, their weight begins to make it crumble. Far away, in the direction Beatrice has gone, he hears her scream. The sound echoes throughout London, a blood-curdling shriek. *The Jacks have her!*

He shouts out loud and comes bolt awake.

He can't sleep after that, and cannot wait for the sun to come up. In fact, it is still dark when he rises from his bed and makes his way to Trafalgar Square to await Dupin. *What happened last night?* Soon the sun peeks over the London skyline. Fat pigeons are about, watched from above by the crows. The vendors won't be here for a couple of hours, but Holmes waits, under the Nelson Monument. The old, legless newsboy sells only one Sunday paper – Sherlock's favorite, the blood-loving *News of the World*. A few folks stroll by, early church bells toll. When Dupin finally arrives he doesn't bear his usual smile. He rolls into the Square on his board, his jaw set and his eyes dead serious. Sherlock sees the other newsboys appearing, every one of them looking somber.

"Mr. Dupin!"

"No joy in London today, Master 'olmes, no joy. They'll be saying prayers in the churches, they will."

"I –"

"I knows what you wants. And I'm 'alf of a mind not to give it to you. Why was you asking about the Spring 'eeled Jack a week ago? What does you know, boy?"

Dupin doesn't sound like his friendly self.

"I know one of the girls who was attacked, that first time. She informed me soon after it happened."

"You means the one the Jack says is next?"

"Next?"

"The one whose door 'ad the note on it."

How does he know that?

"I memorized it, I did, from today's paper. It makes me blood run cold. *I will kill the poor, the 'elpless, the females. Just like our government. I'll start with you. Chaos!* There is an animal, a freak of nature, on the loose in London, Master 'olmes. This ain't like the one I remembers when I was young, or even the one from the Penny Dreadfuls. This one is the devil."

Why did Beatrice give that note to the police? He had specifically told her NOT to. Or did she give it directly to the press? That would be even worse. "What happened last night?"

"You don't know?"

"I know it was terrible, that it was murder."

"It wasn't murder, Master 'olmes, it was *murders*, five of 'em."

Sherlock's heart thumps.

"Five? It killed five people across London?"

"Not across London . . . in just one place. It was a whole family, poor as church mice: the father, the mother . . . and three children, all little girls. It was 'orrible."

Sherlock is speechless. *Could Malefactor do that? And if it wasn't him, then who is this despicable fiend?*

"What is our world coming to? It's days like this that makes you feel it is falling apart. The government 'as to respond to this, Master 'olmes, the Jack is forcing them. Mr. Disraeli, 'es being tested. It's as though this Jack is saying that if the politicians won't 'elp the poor more . . . 'e'll kill 'em all. It's blackmail and terror. 'ere's the paper. No charge.

I'd like to get them off me 'ands today. It's like they is full of blood. When you read this, it will make you sick."

Sherlock takes the paper. The story isn't difficult to find. It screams across the front page.

EVIL IN THE ISLE OF DOGS

A most heinous crime occurred last night in the marshes on the Isle of Dogs. After the sun had descended, a fiend dressed as the Spring Heeled Jack attacked and brutally murdered a family of five. They were residents of nearby Millwall, living in the shacks on Maria Street, the father, Mr. Treasure, a part-time employee of the local rope factory, his wife a seamstress. It is a rough, industrial area, south of the West and East India docks, near the construction location for the new Millwall pool. There are patches of crude homes amongst the factories and shipping wharves, and great stretches of deserted land and black mud. Police seldom patrol there. The Force believe Mr. Treasure was attacked and killed on the doorstep of his little home, which was then entered by the villain, who knocked the wife and little girls insensible and, with fiendish strength, dragged them all out into the marshes in the center of the peninsula. Screams were heard and trails of blood were discovered near the Iron Works, the Lead Works, and the rope-walk that leads to the marsh. Though much blood was found (in fact, it saturated the lying water in the area and turned it red) the bodies were not recovered. It is believed that the fiend butchered them and threw them into the Thames at the Blackwall Reach.

A note was recovered, which the police have not allowed the press to see. One assumes it said something further about killing London's poor, and its females, until the government does more to help them. It seems a vicious and backwards way to go about being of service to the unfortunate.

Mr. Disraeli, who has been avoiding comment on other attacks, will almost certainly be addressing this incident in the Commons today. If he does not, Mr. Bright shall surely force him.

There were two other Spring Heeled Jack attacks last night, without injury, in working-class areas. Both times the fiend materialized briefly and instantly vanished. The police do not know if these appearances were perpetrated by the same beast responsible for brutalizing the Treasure family.

Sherlock looks up, feeling numb. *This doesn't seem real.* He sees another man reading the same story not far away. The man looks shocked, his face as white as a Mayfair bedsheet. The boy turns back to his own newspaper. It has one more paragraph.

It is also rumored that a revolver was stolen from a desk at Scotland Yard some time yesterday. The news that some villain, perhaps this murderous one, may have infiltrated the inner sanctum of our Force does little to alleviate the fear now gripping our streets.

It's like one more blow in the stomach. And then his eyes fall on another report on the front page: of a bomb going off in a suburb, the act attributed to the Irish Fenians, those experts in terror, who are using fear to force the government to give Ireland its independence.

It takes Sherlock a few seconds to be able to move. There aren't many people in the square at this hour, but as he makes his way toward a stone bench, he notices that others who have newspapers are also staring at the front pages in disbelief. He shoves his copy of *The News of the World* into his coat pocket and slouches down onto the bench.

Using Beatrice as bait, not an idea he was entirely comfortable with in the first place, is now impossible. The police will be watching the hatter's shop like hunting dogs, likely stationing a half-dozen men there. Malefactor may not know that Sherlock was with Lestrade last night, but he *might*, and if the Jack is indeed one of his people, then it saw Holmes at the railway bridge. Sherlock glances around the square – *he would be after me with all his might – I may be next*. The boy has no real evidence that connects the Irregulars to this crime and even if he did, he doubts Inspector Lestrade would listen to him. He would be more apt to find a way to arrest him.

Bell always gives the boy Sunday mornings off. He can go where he wants, do what he must do. He sits on the bench, immobile. *Perhaps I should simply hide.* Beatrice is safe now – she doesn't need his protection. *But can I abandon this case?* If Malefactor is indeed behind this Jack, turning angry, murderous, and anxious to contribute to the uneasiness in London, then he must be imprisoned, both for the city's sake . . . and his own. *I must act! But how?*

An hour passes. Various faces and actions involved in the crimes flit across his imagination. He begins to think about Louise. *Who is she? Was there a reason why the Jack attacked her first?* He considers Sigerson Bell's comments about women – *they are more than they seem.*

But at that moment, he is distracted by the sound of drums and bagpipes. It grows louder. The square has been filling up, now it stirs. Rising, the boy sees a mob coming down The Strand, led by men carrying clubs and axes, some holding placards high in the air. "FAIRNESS NOW!" "DOWN WITH THE RICH!" "IRISH SOLIDARITY! MUNBY FOR PM!" And one reads . . . "THE JACK IS RIGHT!" They are singing a union song. Sherlock can't believe how big and disorganized the mob is – this appears to be a spontaneous demonstration. The parade flows from The Strand and across the street into Trafalgar Square, ignoring traffic and bringing it to a halt. As a gentleman in a black top hat passes the demonstrators, a tough-looking protestor shoves him and knocks him to the ground. When two Bobbies approach, they are surrounded and have to fight their way out, running toward nearby White Hall and

Scotland Yard. Gentlemen and ladies – anyone dressed in clothing that looks better than working class – scramble from the square.

"The Jack is a Irishman, I wagers," Sherlock hears a dirty-faced man say. "Me member of Parliament even thinks it is. Said as much. They should round up them Paddies, and beat 'em until one confesses. The Jack wears green on 'is black suit, don't 'e?"

The crowd forms a big circle, and some of the working-class men begin to speak in its center, screaming profane words and abuse directed at the government and the Irish. Some make nasty racial comments about Disraeli. They are calling for violence, for an overthrow of the class system. Sherlock spies Alfred Munby in the mob, trying to blend in and look inconspicuous.

Holmes, wearing his shabby clothes, isn't bothered by anyone. He stands and watches in disbelief. The crowd continues to grow. A lady in a pink hat with flowers and a long pink coat passes in a beautiful barouche carriage, open to the crisp March air. Several men run after her, knock her coachman from his perch and pull her from her seat. She screams as they carry her toward the mob. In a moment she is at its center, alone and weeping. Another man advances and knocks her to the ground.

But at that instant, Sherlock notices a ripple in the crowd. Someone is plowing his way through, shouting at the others and pushing them aside. In a flash, he is at the center of the circle too. He stands between the brute who knocked the woman to the ground and the lady, facing the rough. The crowd gasps and goes silent. It is Robert Hide. He turns to the lady, offers her his hand and helps her to her feet, then nods to three people in the mob and instructs them to return her to her carriage.

Fascinated, Sherlock rushes through the crowd toward the front. He notices John Bright approaching, passes John Bedford Leno, the most important Reform League leader in the nation, rumored to have had a meeting with the Fenians, during which they asked him to help start a Civil War. He claims he wasn't tempted, but many wonder if he's loyal, if he keeps secrets. Sherlock brushes by two men – one well-dressed, his facial hair smoothly groomed and as black as coal, the other a little older, the beard turning white and spreading onto his chest like Father Christmas's – Friedrich Engels and Karl Marx, notorious German authors who live here now and predict the working class will soon rule the world. Bright is pushing toward the front of the crowd, looking concerned.

"London! Listen to me!" shouts Robert Hide. "This is not the way. This is NOT the way!" There are shouts of disapproval but he spins around, glares back at the loudmouths, and silences them. One of his looks is for Alfred Munby. "Change MUST come! But change will come through debate and democracy!" Only a few groans are heard. "Fear is ruling our streets now! *Fear!* But our government has been put on notice! It WILL change! Keep the pressure on the parliamentarians!" A huge cheer goes up. "If they do not respond . . . they *know* the consequences!" An enormous cry of approval cascades over Trafalgar Square.

But as it does, the Force enters the area on horseback. And their steeds are not at a trot; they are galloping. Screams are heard from the back rows and people begin to scatter. Sherlock takes to his heels. He heads for higher ground, toward the National Art Gallery. The mob flees. People run into each other, shouting, pursued by police and horses, Bobbies club protestors with truncheons. Several men knock over a wagon and light it on fire. The flames catch in the wind and shoot high into the air, climbing up the Nelson Monument. Union men try to fight back. Policemen and protestors grapple on the ground. More fires are lit. Chaos descends on the square in the center of London.

As Sherlock looks back, he spots Malefactor in the midst of the mob, walking through it with Grimsby and Crew, calm as the Lake District. He is grinning. His eyes meet Sherlock's and he stops. His smile widens and he points at Holmes and beckons him to come toward him. His look is demonic.

Sherlock turns and runs again. As he approaches the Gallery's stone stairway, he sees Irene standing way up at the top, today dressed more like an actress than the respectable young girl he used to know. Her dress is a loud purple and hugs her frame. It shows her slender wrists and forearms, exposed even on this cool day. Just a light red shawl is thrown over her shoulders and she has put a touch of rouge on her cheeks. But he feels sorry for her – she looks terri-fied. He rushes up the stairs to her.

"Sherlock, what is happening?"

"You must get out of here!"

"Was that Mr. Hide? Was he speaking?"

"He was trying to subdue them."

"Is that Malefactor?"

"You must get out of here. *Now!*"

He takes her hand and ushers her to a place beside the Gallery's tall front doors, behind the pillars, away from the crowd. Within minutes, down below, the police begin to gain control of things. The crowd is being dispersed. Several wagons from the London Fire Brigade have arrived and are putting out the flames. Malefactor stands in the center of the square, Grimsby and Crew on either side, staring up the steps toward Sherlock and Irene.

Holmes returns the look. He waits a little longer for the area to clear more and then descends the steps with Irene, stomping directly toward his enemy. Church bells are tolling in the distance. The police, noticing the eccentrically dressed boy's companion, allow them to enter the square. Malefactor begins to look uneasy.

Sherlock drags Irene right up to him and the two boys confront each other, almost surrounded by the police. Grimsby and Crew close ranks and stand closer to their boss.

"I know ALL about you!"

"Keep your voice down, Jew-boy," says Malefactor, through his clenched teeth.

"Hear this. And you hear it too, Miss Doyle." He steps right up to Malefactor. "You are a two-faced fake. You tell made-up stories about your past to Irene. Even your life here on the streets is a lie."

Malefactor glances toward Irene and back at Sherlock.

"Last night, I followed you through the streets to Lincoln's Inn Fields. I was with the boy your little thugs hanged upside down from the lamppost."

"I have no idea what you –"

"And I saw you all in that semi-circle . . . while one of your number dressed up as the Spring Heeled Jack!"

"I –"

"I am guessing it was this over-sized pig, Crew – the one with the beautiful black hair."

The big lad is impassive, but Grimsby steps forward, his fists balled. Malefactor instantly places his cane across the smaller boy's throat, holding him back. He glances up at a nearing Bobbie on horseback.

"You are mistaken."

"About Crew? Or all of it? I *know* one of you dressed up as the Jack. Don't deny it."

"Is that true, Malefactor?" asks Irene.

"Irene, you know Holmes doesn't like me. We have discussed this before."

"Is it true? Do NOT lie to me."

"Only partially."

"A family was murdered last night, an entire family!" cries Irene. "Three little girls!" She steps closer to Sherlock.

"And I, Miss Doyle, had nothing to do with it, on my honor."

"Your honor!"

"Close your mouth, Holmes, or you will regret it!"

"What do you mean by that?" asks Irene.

"I mean, simply, Miss Doyle, that he is in error. And were he to pursue a case against me, he would have occasion to regret it because the police would discover my innocence. Yes, we dressed up Crew as the Jack. But we were just having fun. I contributed to the Spring Heeled scare because I am an anarchist . . . that is my political philosophy. There are many interesting folks, Radicals, with similar ideas. We had NOTHING to do with the murders. You know, Miss Doyle, that I would not do that . . . that I would not harm little girls."

"I believe you."

"And I do *not*."

"You are welcome then, Master Holmes, to examine the costume we used. You are welcome to take it, and us, to Scotland Yard, and discover if anything at the crime scene matches anything to do with us. I make that offer knowing well the implicit danger into which it puts me and my faithful company."

Lestrade might laugh me out of the building.

Irene smiles and looks to Sherlock. "Satisfied? I understand that Malefactor is not perfect, and he and I disagree about many things. But I think, Master Holmes, that he has proven something to you just now."

Sherlock is glaring at his rival. "You cannot deny that you promised to kill me."

"I can. That is a fantasy; your problem, not mine. You have a fevered imagination. You do not like what I do or my philosophy, so you make it much worse, and invent horrible things that are not true. The world is a difficult place and I participate as best I can, but I am not a savage."

"Have you ever been to Queens Gardens?"

Malefactor's face turns white. He becomes mute.

"Sir?" asks Grimsby.

"Stand here now," continues Sherlock, "and tell Miss Doyle to her face that everything you told her about your past is true."

"COME!" screams Malefactor, seizing both his lieutenants by their coats and pushing them away. "We must be off! On the double!"

"Malefactor?" asks Irene. "What does this mean? Answer him."

But the criminal has shoved the other two thugs hard, sent them sprawling away, and turned away himself. As he starts to run, they run with him. When he gets to the far end of the square, he looks back and catches Sherlock's eye. It is an expression that would freeze the devil.

"I don't know who to believe anymore," says Irene, looking stunned. "You or him or my father, or . . . anyone, even Robert Hide. I think . . . I just need to believe in myself."

Sherlock must reach out to her. Now is the time – she seems ready to reject Malefactor. But as he steps toward her, he sees someone scurrying across the square close by, whose very presence stops him.

"Beatrice?"

At first, the hatter's daughter acts as if she doesn't hear him, but she then comes to a halt.

"Sherlock 'olmes?"

"Who is that?" asks Irene.

"A friend of mine."

"A friend? She's pretty."

"I . . . I hadn't noticed."

Beatrice looks at Irene and her attractive dress and then glances down at her own, tattered and stained. She fixes her hair, falling out as it is from her brown bonnet. "I . . . I must be going," she says, and darts away. Sherlock wonders if she was here when the riot happened. He hopes she was spared it.

"So must I," says Irene, and stomps away.

He is left alone in Trafalgar Square. He wants to run after them, but doesn't know which one to pursue. He wishes he could be in two places at once.

He tells himself to stop thinking about them. Irene has changed; and Beatrice is protected now. Suddenly, there is no reason to think about the Spring Heeled Jack anymore either – Malefactor is a liar, but Sherlock doesn't believe he is lying about the murders. He would never offer to go to the police with his Jack's costume if he were guilty of that gruesome crime. It doesn't make sense. These latest attacks don't seem like his enemy's style anyway. Not clever enough.

I have no stake in this anymore. Best to let the authorities deal with it. But London is nearly in flames. Can I just sit by and watch?

"Sherlock?"

He has been standing alone in the center of the square for much longer than he realizes – the fires smoldering around him, the crowd gone, just a few policemen left, Irene and Beatrice long vanished. He didn't notice the figure approaching him . . . but then, this person is good at sneaking up on people.

"Master Lestrade . . . you startled me."

"I was just coming to Denmark Street to see you."

"I believe our score is two to one on startling one another of late. That's in my favor."

The young detective-in-training suppresses a smile. He doesn't appear to be in a mood to laugh. In fact, he looks terrible. And Sherlock has the sense that it isn't entirely about the riot.

"Coming to see me? Well, I just happened to meet Miss Leckie – much more interesting for you to speak with her. She went that way." He points south. "You could probably catch up to –"

"No, I want to see you." The look on his face grows darker. It scares Sherlock.

"About what?"

"About this." He takes a piece of paper from his pocket. "I went with my father to the crime scene. It was horrible. There was so much blood. I . . . I saw a tiny photograph of the three little girls . . . in their hovel. It was lying on the dirt floor near the straw that they use to sleep on. The frame was smashed and it was covered with blood." He looks down at the paper again. "I . . . I don't know how

I was able to find this when my father couldn't. I was outside, between the house and the marsh. It was crumpled up, as if it had fallen out of someone's pocket."

"What is it?"

"I didn't show it to my father. I promise."

He holds the paper so Sherlock can read it. It is splattered with scarlet. Though it is difficult to tell, the note looks as though it is written in the same hand used on the villain's other two messages – the one left on Louise Stevenson and the one on Beatrice's door.

The boy reads it.

SHERLOCK HOLMES ON OUR SIDE.

16

THE FLIGHT OF LOUISE STEVENSON

"I can't keep this from my father for long. It is my duty to show him."

"Thank you. But you don't think that –"

"I will give you twenty-four hours to either leave London for good . . . or help me catch the fiend who murdered that family."

"I –"

"If I am empty handed at the end of that time, I will make up a story that I went back to the crime scene and found it then. When I show it to Father, he will pursue you until he catches you. And he will. I must soon reveal this, Master Holmes. This fiend is a savage killer. I cannot withhold evidence. I cannot play with people's lives."

"Surely, you don't truly suspect me. That's absurd!"

"Is it?"

"You know me."

"Do I? Do I really, Sherlock? Think about it. Even if we were close friends, what would I know about you that matters? My father often talks about people being shocked when a neighbor commits a crime. *He seemed like such a nice man* . . . they always say that."

"But –"

"What is going on in my mind right now, for example?"

Sherlock examines him, but Lestrade cuts him off.

"Don't try, Holmes. I know you are a self-described genius of observation, you have parlor tricks that help you tell others all about themselves, their heritage, their home, whether they are left-handed or right . . . that they live in Hounslow. But you cannot tell me what I feel. You cannot tell me if, deep down, I am actually a terrible person or a saint, what I harbor deep in my soul."

Sherlock can't disagree.

"I do not *know* that you are not helping this fiend, that you are not in fact, the Spring Heeled Jack himself. You play with fire, Holmes, you love exploring criminality . . . perhaps it has excited you too much? They say that villains, in the end, are more interesting than rest of us. Perhaps you've given in to the thrill of –"

"No, Lestrade. No, it doesn't excite me. It *never* will."

"I'm not sure I believe you. But . . . I will trust you to the degree that I will give you a chance to prove otherwise. Most in my position wouldn't even do that. I may be making a terrible mistake. I will give you twenty-four hours. That's all I can allow. Tomorrow, Monday, at noon, I shall go to my father with this note."

He is holding it up, extending it toward Sherlock, who reaches for it so he can examine it more closely. Lestrade snaps it away and puts it into his pocket.

"When you have something, anything, let me know immediately."

He walks away, across the smoldering square toward Scotland Yard.

Sherlock's mind is racing. *Twenty-four hours.* His entire way of life could soon be over. He knows nothing about the identity of the Spring Heeled Jack. Finding him in a day seems impossible. Perhaps, given the odds, it would be smart to spend his time readying himself to depart, packing up, speaking to Sigerson Bell, going south to the Crystal Palace to talk to his father. Saying good-bye to Irene . . . and Beatrice.

When he thinks of Miss Leckie, he is reminded of Louise Stevenson, and that gives him a tiny spark of energy, turns his mind back to the crimes. *She is more than she seems . . . as most women are.* Sherlock wonders. *Should I make enquiries about her?* He can't give up. He thinks of his mother. He can't give up on her and on what he believes he must do with his life.

There is more than Louise to investigate, he tells himself, trying to gather more energy. *I must look at that note, examine it carefully. What about Malefactor? Could he be forced to help?*

"Lestrade!"

The other boy hears the shout at the far end of Trafalgar Square. He waits as Sherlock runs up to him.

"Care for a stroll?"

Yesterday, Sherlock hadn't told Lestrade exactly where Malefactor lived. He merely mentioned that he resided in Knightsbridge and then asked him to wait for him at the Wellington Arch.

"You have twenty-four hours. You should be –"

"Malefactor lives in a large white house in Queens Gardens in Knightsbridge. He knows as much about the criminal underworld as anyone in the city. Though I am now certain he or one of his colleagues is not the Spring Heeled Jack we seek, I am guessing he would have a great deal to contribute concerning the possible identity of the villain. He may not know exactly who he is, but he likely has an idea, and if he doesn't, he knows people who will put us on the right track."

"But why would he tell us anything?"

"Because I will knock on his door, his secret hiding place, with the son of the senior police inspector of Scotland Yard by my side. What secrets are inside those doors? We can threaten to reveal all about him, and not just to the police, but to his evil little cohorts, who appear to know nothing of his double life."

"Blackmail?"

"Blackmail."

Sherlock figures that he was in the square for more than an hour after the riot, and that it will take them more than half an hour to get to Queens Gardens. He is guessing that his sudden revelation spooked Malefactor, that he rushed home to get ready to leave . . . or that he is staying away from home, planning to sneak in late at night and prepare his departure. He and Lestrade shall either catch him at home or force the door . . . and wait for him inside. Holmes shall rip that beard from his face!

"Master Lestrade," says Sherlock after they have been walking in silence for a few moments, "I see you have that magnifying glass with you."

The other boy's face colors a little. He not only took to carrying a glass because he had seen Sherlock using one a few months ago, but Holmes has the infuriating habit of knowing when it is on his person, by identifying the bulge in his coat pocket. Today he had pushed it farther down and thought he had disguised its presence.

"Yes, I do."

"May I examine the note with it?"

"No, you may not."

Holmes stops. "Why not?"

"Because I do not trust you. You shall steal the note and make a run for it."

"Then allow me a moment with the glass, examining the note whilst you hold it in your forever trustworthy hands."

They are at St. James's Park. Lestrade walks over to a bench, Sherlock following, sits down, pulls out the glass, hands it over, and holds up the red-stained note. After Holmes's momentary examination, they are on their way again. Neither boy says anything for awhile. Lestrade smiles.

"Nothing I didn't notice?"

"Nothing. I must apologize."

Three remnants of horse hairs on the note; blood a strange color, not clotting in the usual way.

Just past Hyde Park Corner, seemingly out of the blue, Sherlock asks a question. "Did you find this note on a roadway?"

"No, it was out in the marsh. I told you that."

"Are you sure?"

"Of course I am sure."

"Do horses frequent the marsh?"

"Horses? What an absurd question. A horse would get stuck and have to be shot out there. Only an imbecile would take one to the marsh."

"Not something you would do, then?"

"Watch your mouth, Holmes. . . . What are you driving at? Did you find some evidence on the note?"

"Not a thing. My head is empty. I cannot wait to unmask Malefactor."

But when they get to Queens Gardens, the shutters are neither open nor closed. There are no shutters at all!

"Sherlock . . . are you, sure this is the place?"

They notice a well-dressed man coming out the front door.

"Excuse me, sir," says Lestrade, "is the gentleman who lives here at home?"

"No one lives here, my good fellow. Not anymore."

"But –"

"I am the house agent." The man offers a winning smile. "And this magnificent residence is for sale. For sale, I say, not to be let. Most houses in this neighborhood are leased, you know. Not this noble abode." He motions to it with an extravagant hand gesture. "Are your parents interested in a new home?"

Lestrade looks indignant.

"Messrs. Henry & Edward, Auctioneers and Agents,

at your service." His smile somehow broadens. "In the bow windows of our establishment on Lanyon Street, you shall soon read of this mansion's charms: gas laid on, carriage drive, four bedrooms, drawing rooms, library, servants' quarters below the –"

"We do not want to purchase," interjects Sherlock. "We know the owner."

The house agent looks Holmes up and down. His smile dissolves and is replaced by a sneer. At first it seems as though he won't deign to answer, but finally he speaks, addressing Lestrade.

"Actually, I barely made his acquaintance. A youngish man with an enormous, black beard, almost too large for his age?"

"That's him," says Sherlock. "We are here to see him on important business."

"Then, you must seek him elsewhere. We received a note about an hour ago, telling us to meet him here. It was the most extraordinary thing. The note asked if we would pay him exactly half of what this house is worth and that we could keep the profit when we sold it. I was to bring him bank notes and come instantly. We, of course, were happy to oblige. When I arrived, he had three wagons on the street and they were already loaded with furniture and other household effects. The house is quite bare inside. I saw him only briefly. He had to sign a contract, which he was reluctant to do, but finally relented. He left about twenty minutes ago."

"What name did he use?" asks Holmes.

"Use?"

"I have known him for many years, but not his last name. I am curious."

"Well, to be honest, I'm not sure I know that either. His signature is difficult to read. He was in a hurry, and I didn't ask questions. Why should I? He gave us the deed, my friends." Another smile. "There was the same scrawl there. I suppose there's no harm in you looking. It's right here."

The house agent pulls the contract out of his pocket. Sherlock examines the name.

It is indeed impossible to decipher. But he can tell it isn't Malefactor, at least not exactly. It has the same number of syllables, starts with an *M* . . . but ends with a *Y*.

"I hate to interrupt," says Master Lestrade. When Sherlock turns to him, he sees that the other boy is angry. "We must be on our way." A dozen steps down the street toward Brompton Road, Lestrade explodes at Holmes.

"We spoke of imbeciles a short time ago. *That* was an imbecile's errand! You are wasting your time and mine! I hope your next idea, if you have any others, is a better one. Twenty-four hours! No . . ." he pulls out his pocket watch, "less than twenty-three!"

He walks briskly away, leaving Sherlock standing on Brompton Road. The boy has a decision to make. Malefactor has gone underground, the horse hair and unusual blood on the note are nothing but strange facts . . . and time has already begun to run out.

Shall I go home and prepare to leave? Or try my one last idea? Louise.

When Sherlock went to visit Beatrice shortly after the first attack, she had spoken a little about her life over the last few months, as she explained how she and Louise ended up on Westminster Bridge late at night, set upon by the Spring Heeled Jack. She had talked about her new employment, though she didn't reveal that she sought the job because her father had fallen on hard times. Now, when Sherlock thinks of it, the frequent absence of Mr. Leckie from Southwark should have spoken volumes about their situation. Her father, not well to begin with, was obviously seeking other work, probably something menial and even more dangerous to his health. Part of the reason this hadn't occurred to Sherlock was that Beatrice had spoken so cheerfully of her work, as if it were enjoyable, and a new challenge. She told him where she and Louise were employed and even described the house – on a grand street in Kensington, just west of Knightsbridge.

Sherlock makes up his mind. He will try this one last thing. If it leads nowhere, he will be gone by the morning. He runs all the way to Kensington and finds the mansion, its appearance just as Beatrice said. He paces back and forth in front of it several times, trying to look inconspicuous, but the only employees he sees are footmen, who twice answer the door. That won't do. He cannot ask them about another servant, cannot take the risk of being suspected of something. He must speak to someone more lowly, and female. After a half-dozen more passes, the last few drawing looks from passersby, he spots a girl in a servant's black dress and white apron and bonnet, not much older than Beatrice, rushing out from the rear below-ground door of the house to the street, snapping a couple of coins into her little purse. Sherlock stands up straight and tries to add a few years to his age. He will lower his voice a little too. *A scullery maid, like Beatrice, at the bottom of the pecking order. About seventeen years old. She's on an errand. One button purposely undone at the top of her dress, pinching her cheeks to make them rosy; likes the opposite sex a little more than she should.*

"Excuse me?"

At first, she looks apprehensive.

"What do you want?"

"Louise Stevenson."

"Oh you does, does you?" She smiles.

"Just –"

"You a bit young for 'er, ain't you?"

"I am just a friend . . . though I could be more."

"Yes, I'm sure you could, you young rascal."

"I would like to bring her a flower . . . to her home. I have a song to sing for her too."

"Well, to it then, lad. Why is you standing 'ere? Or should you like to sing for me?"

"But I don't know where she lives. We've just met."

She looks suspicious. "And 'ow does I know you ain't some fiend? Maybe you is the Spring 'eeled Jack! Attacked 'er, 'e did, you know. Made her famous. 'e only attacks the ladies, us poor ones, they says. I 'ear 'e is kinda 'andsome . . . 'andsome and dangerous." She giggles.

"I am not the Spring Heeled Jack, my lady. I have no secrets, other than my affection for Miss Stevenson, which I would like to make known to her."

"Well, ain't you the talker. Tell me somethin' about 'er that makes me believe you ain't just wantin' to 'urt 'er. 'Cause you know, if you is unsuited for 'er, I is available. I likes that talk 'o yours, all proper and refined-like. Very nice. Out with it! What do you knows of 'er?"

"She is a close friend of Beatrice Leckie, who is employed here as well, and lives in the Mint area in Southwark, daughter of a hatter."

"You sure you wouldn't prefer me, 'andsome?"

"If it weren't for Miss Stevenson, I would."

"Oh! You is *such* a talker!" She slaps him lightly on the shoulder. "Miss Stevenson lives in Limehouse, though I tell you, I've been there once or twice and it ain't very nice in those parts. I'm 'appy I live in with the lady and gentleman 'ere. The Stevensons is awfully poor. Her father worked in a 'orse glue factory in Rotherhithe direct across the river, but the Duke who owned it, 'e closed it down because, they said, 'e didn't like the color of the glue. 'er father 'ad inhaled the chemicals in there for many a year. 'is lungs don't work right now. 'e can't get work no longer."

"What is the address, if you please?"

"On Samoa Street, off Narrow Road, right near the river. It ain't much of a street. Just ask anyone who lives there for the family."

It takes Sherlock more than an hour to get to Limehouse. As he walks at a brisk pace, he continues to consider what he knows about the case. He has very little, almost nothing. Then a thought occurs to him. He has seen all three notes. *The handwriting! That's at least something. It was the same on every one. If I could find the hand that wrote it, and look up that arm to the face . . . I would have my solution.* It's an intriguing idea, but virtually impossible to follow through on.

Limehouse is east of Stepney, past the area where little Paul Doyle used to live in the workhouse. Many of its streets are populated with the desperately poor, with seafaring men and their families, living many people to a room. Samoa Street is no exception. The buildings are jammed together. Sherlock keeps alert, his wits about him, remembering his Bellitsu defenses. Once he gets to Narrow Road, he asks a child, running about in bare feet in the March weather, where he might find the Stevensons. He is directed to their rough little home, the ground floor of a slim, brick building.

The man who answers the door is coughing into a cloth. There are red splats on it. He is obviously Mr. Stevenson, probably in his forties, though he looks closer to seventy. The boy spots Louise sitting at a little table in the only room that is evident, conversing with her haggard-looking mother and six other children. There is a fireplace and five beds crammed against the walls. Everyone stops talking the instant he appears, though he hears a little of what is being said, and thinks Louise mentions Alfred

Munby. She stands up with a start when she sees Sherlock Holmes, shoving her chair back. Before her father can question the visitor, she has wrapped a ragged shawl around her shoulders, come forward, and ushered Sherlock out the door and into the street.

"Master 'olmes, what a surprise." She is trying to sound pleased, but rushing him down the road away from the house, as if they are meant to walk out together.

"Miss Stevenson, shouldn't I meet your family? Or are you ashamed of me?"

"Now, Master 'olmes, what a thing to say, I –"

"Then, why didn't you offer proper introductions? Why are we talking in the street? Is that the correct manner in which to treat a caller?"

"It's because . . . because of the Spring 'eeled Jack."

"Yes?"

"I . . . uh . . . knows you are 'ere to ask about it, I'm sure. I don't want to concern them about such things. They is very fragile."

"Well, you are correct. That *is* why I have come to see you."

"Does that mean you is going to look into things? That is wonderful, Master 'olmes! Beatrice will be pleased. She thinks so 'ighly of you, sir. Talks of you non-stop, says you could find this fiend. Do you have any clues?"

"Yes. I have one."

"And can you tell a lard-headed girl like me 'bout it?"

"Yes, I can. In fact, I must. You, Miss Stevenson, are my clue."

She turns white. "I beg your pardons, Master 'olmes?"

"Why did the Jack attack you?"

"Well, sir, you asked me that before, I'm sure you did, and I 'ave no answer. 'ow could I?"

"Who are you, Louise?"

"Who am I?" She blanches again. "What a question. Well, sure, I am Louise Stevenson, a poor girl, a friend of Beatrice Leckie's, and an unfortunate victim of the Jack."

"Hardly a victim, you didn't suffer a scratch, and he had a good deal of time to do you harm. Who do you know whom the Jack might know? I overheard you mention Alfred Munby. Don't deny it."

Louise swallows. "I don't know 'im, 'onest. I am sure I knows no one. I . . . I must be going."

Holmes grabs her by the arm. He raises his voice. "If you know anything about this that you haven't told me or the police, you had best tell me now! Do you know the evil that was done last night? Have you read the newspapers?" Sherlock pulls *The News of the World* from his pocket and wields it, almost as if he is about to hit her with it. A burly sailor, grimy from head to foot and smelling of ale, passes by.

"Is you all right, miss?" He glares at Sherlock.

"I am fine, sir, thank you. This gentleman meant nothing by it. 'e is about to escort me 'ome and be on 'is way."

The sailor walks slowly away, looking back at Holmes

"You are 'urting me, Sherlock." Her voice sounds different. There is an edge in it, a hint of anger, almost as if she is threatening him with the sailor, or something else, if he doesn't let go.

He releases her arm.

"I ask you again. Have you read the newspapers? Do you know what he did?"

"I can't read, Master 'olmes."

An hour later, Sherlock Holmes is still on Samoa Street. After escorting Louise back to her home, he had walked up the road away from the river and found an indented doorway in an abandoned stone building with boards over its windows. He sat down in it, out of the way, looking like a beggar, his eyes cast down the street toward the Stevenson home. He had seen fear in Louise's face when he questioned her, especially when he asked if she knew anyone who had anything to do with these crimes. He thinks she has secrets and has made a calculation. He predicts that in a short while she will be leaving her house. Where she goes will tell him a good deal about the identity of the Spring Heeled Jack. He remembers Alfred Munby's dark face at the riot in Trafalgar Square.

Louise Stevenson is guilty of something. Exactly what, he isn't sure. But he does know this – she could not have written those notes. *She cannot read.*

Just a short while later, he sees her emerge. She has put on her coat, tied her bonnet down tightly, and after glancing up and down the street, heads south, toward the river. Sherlock follows. Miss Stevenson will be moving on foot – she doesn't have money for a cab. Not that cabs are often seen in this part of Limehouse, anyway.

At first, he thinks she is going somewhere back in central London. She scurries down to Narrow Street, passes by the Jolly Hangman Tavern, and heads west along the Thames. He follows her for a long time. They pass sailors, dock workers, wharves, ships under construction, and rope factories. Just beyond the London Docks, she pauses at the Thames Tunnel, the dark subterranean passage under the river, as if debating whether or not to enter it alone. After a while, she moves on, until she comes to London Bridge. Once over it, he expects her to make for the hatter's shop, but she doesn't. She turns east and hurries down river toward Rotherhithe.

This was where Sherlock helped capture the notorious Brixton Gang last year. Though he is proud of what he did, he has no stomach for returning today. It is an industrial wasteland, full of docks and crime. But he can't let Louise out of his sight. He is amazed that she would come here.

She keeps her head down and ignores the catcalls from roughs who see her. Sherlock prays he doesn't have to intercede. But she actually barks back at some of the men who taunt her from the doors of taverns and factories, despite their size and violent attitude. Sherlock can barely keep up with her. He continues to expect her to stop, but on and on she goes, past the Whiting Asphalte Works, the warehouse where Sherlock found the gang, down past the Limehouse Reach, and out of Rotherhithe by King's Yard (where the Royal Navy's ships are built), then veers slightly away from the Thames and into Deptford. By the time they get there, they have been walking for more than an hour and she is still maintaining her aggressive pace. Louise Stevenson certainly isn't what she seems. Under that humble exterior there is obviously an extraordinary toughness, and under that dress a pair of unusually strong legs. *What is she up to?*

They have come so far that they are now in London's suburbs. Greenwich appears. This is a much nicer area, hilly and beautiful with bigger homes and many parks. To the north is Greenwich Hospital, the former site of a country palace where kings used to ride to the hounds, where Sir Walter Raleigh famously laid down his cape over a muddy puddle to keep Queen Elizabeth's shoes from being soiled. The dirt is black and rich, the coming spring evident in the open green areas and sprouting trees. It actually seems warmer here, as if God heats it especially for its residents. *What business does Louise Stevenson have here?*

She swings south of the Royal Observatory in huge tree-lined Greenwich Park and approaches Blackheath. Sherlock can feel blisters on his toes, but Louise doesn't seem to be suffering at all. Her head is up now, in this much safer area, her nose pointing toward her destination. Holmes senses that they are nearing it.

Blackheath Village is a gorgeous little spot with its own shops and businesses, a kind of haven just outside of London. John Stuart Mill lives here . . . the great man, not the dog. Birds are singing, people are strolling about on the little streets, governesses push prams, well-dressed children dutifully by their sides. It is like a painting from a storybook that starts and ends very well.

Louise turns down a smaller road off the main street.

She looks just as out of place as her pursuer. Though the houses are a good size here, they aren't enormous, not like those in Mayfair or Belgravia. But there is a lovely home-spun feel to them. They are relatively new, with cream or white stucco exteriors, large latticed windows, and fake thatched roofs. Louise stops at one. It has beautiful pink blossoms just beginning on the small apple trees on the front lawn, which is surrounded by a white picket fence. Holmes sees a long low building at the rear, attached to the house. Louise hesitates then swings the gate open. It creaks. She moves slowly up the walkway. A figure appears at the front window, and then comes to the door and opens it. The boy is careful to stay well down the street, out of sight. Whoever has come to the door is greeting Louise happily, as if she is an old friend. It is a man. Sherlock steps into the street to see who it is.

Robert Hide.

17

DEAD END

Sherlock Holmes is not used to running out of ideas. But here he is, across the street from Robert Hide's surprisingly idyllic home far from the troubles of downtown London, and he does not know what to do. If he had more time, he would retreat now, go back to the apothecary shop, maybe consult Sigerson Bell, gather his thoughts, and concoct a scheme. That would be the prudent – the scientific – way to proceed. But he doesn't have *any* time. The sun is beginning to set and the village, equipped with just a few gas lamps, is growing darker. Before noon tomorrow, he must know the identity of the Spring Heeled Jack. His only clue is in the person of Louise Stevenson, and she is in that house across the street consulting one of London's most powerful reformers. It would, perhaps, be best if he waited for her to come out. But he doesn't know if he can afford to even pause. A few more minutes pass, and she is still inside. He begins to think that it may be better to confront them together, anyway. If they are guilty of something, he might spook them, put them off their guard. *Make people ill at ease and you can extract things from them all that much easier.* He wishes he had his horsewhip. He recalls Hide's thick chest and arms, the fact that at twenty-two, he is in the prime of his life.

The boy takes a deep breath and gets up from behind the post in the little driveway down the street. He strides over to Hide's house, swings open the creaking white gate, and is about to pound on the door when he realizes he can hear voices inside.

He puts his ear to the door, but he can't make out what is being said. Then he hears two words very clearly.

"Sherlock Holmes."

There is silence. He raises his fist to bang on the door, but suddenly, it opens. Robert Hide is standing there, his expression as serene as ever, a smile growing on his face, a truly handsome and charismatic man. He is wearing a mousy gray dressing gown, red Persian slippers, and holds a black pipe in his hand. Behind him, Louise Stevenson appears in the front hallway just beyond the vestibule, her bonnet still on. She puts her hand to her mouth in shock.

"You followed me?"

"Yes, as a matter of fact, I did."

"Won't you come in?" asks Hide politely.

Should I? "Yes . . . yes, I will." He marches into the house. A rich, red Indian rug stretches along the hall floor. The walls are gleaming mahogany. A huge grandfather clock stands nearby, ticking quietly. He can see another room to his right, filled with paintings.

"What is the meaning of this?" demands Sherlock.

"Won't you come into the morning room and sit down?" inquires Hide with a smile. "We can best chat in there. I believe we have met, have we not?"

He remembers me? He met me once, for a brief moment.

"I make it my business to remember faces. I believe you are skilled in that sort of thing as well, Master Holmes?"

"I . . . yes . . . I have been taught to be observant. . . . I don't need to sit down. I am fine right here. I would like an explanation."

"Master 'olmes, you must leave and go –"

"Nonsense, Miss Stevenson. Master Holmes is welcome to stay."

Sherlock regards him. He is difficult to read. All the boy can see is an attractive, dark-haired young man with an honest smile, betraying – nothing.

"You were asking the meaning of this? I believe that was the way you put it?"

"Yes. Yes, I was."

"To be honest, I am not exactly sure what you mean by that. But please explain and I shall answer you as best I can."

"This young woman was attacked by the Spring Heeled Jack while in the company of one of my dear friends, Miss Beatrice Leckie. Though I would prefer to stay out of such things, I have become deeply involved in the pursuit of the fiend. The original attack does not make sense. Miss Stevenson has some explaining to do. I followed her here. Why, sir, is this working-class girl from Limehouse, who has had this unique experience, coming to you in Blackheath

Village directly after I questioned her on the subject – directly after she tried to evade my inquiries and looked frightened by them? Why did she fly to you?"

"Well, I know she was the unfortunate victim of that despicable villain's first assault. Though I have not had the good fortune of meeting Miss Leckie, Miss Stevenson, who –"

"I need a direct answer, sir. A family was brutally murdered by the Jack just last night, you must know that. This is not just some passing concern!"

"Yes, Master Holmes, I am well aware of that." His voice almost breaks. "In fact, the Treasure family was known to me. They attended my rallies . . . spoke to me. They, like Miss Stevenson, shared my political views. . . . You seem surprised about Louise, Master Holmes, but she is not what she seems." He smiles at Sherlock. "She has given a good deal of thought to what she thinks her country should be and do. I would be proud to have her as a fellow voter."

Sherlock regards Louise, who stares back at him defiantly. Any trace of a poor innocent girl has vanished from her face.

"With all due respect, Miss Stevenson can't even read."

"And neither, in essence, can many of our Members of Parliament. They cannot read the writing on the wall. Miss Stevenson, on the other hand, understands what must be done in England. When there are many millions like her, things shall change. Forever. Had the Treasure family not been forced to live in such squalor, perhaps they would not have become this maniac's victims. Miss Stevenson is fighting for the likes of them."

"I have known Mr. 'ide for a long –"

Hide raises his hand to her. It is the first time Sherlock has seen him look even the tiniest bit perturbed.

"I shall explain, Miss Stevenson, if I might? I will answer his question, directly."

"Yes, Robert, of course."

"I had seen this lovely young lady many times at my meetings –"

"With Beatrice?" asks Sherlock.

"I believe I mentioned that I am not acquainted with Miss Leckie."

"Beatrice is a fine soul," interjects Louise, "finer than any of us. She is above politics, just an honest child . . . who cares for you, Master Holmes . . . though I'm not sure why." She gives him another look. Sherlock has noticed that her accent seems much improved.

Who is she? Who is this young woman? "As I was saying," continues Hide, "Miss Stevenson came to me at the meeting in Trafalgar Square, after she was attacked, and asked me to help her. She was traumatized by the assault, and at her wits' end. I am afraid that all I could offer was comfort."

"Not like you, Sherlock Holmes," spits Louise, "who thought the assault a farce!"

"I have my methods, Miss Stevenson, and they pointed to such a conclusion."

"You cared about as much for me and what happened to me as you likely do about the poor of this country, the working people, and women! Half of this nation is starving or ill-fed or dying of heartbreak! When they lose their jobs,

jobs the upper classes give and take on whims, they lose their lives and their families! The government sits by idly and lets it happen! Most people in this country still do not even have the right to vote – to change things! Women, if we were given power, would turn this nation upside down!"

Hide smiles. "Miss Stevenson, though I quite agree with you, this may not be the time for such a political discussion. I am sure that Master Holmes is not without feelings for the poor. I understand that you, sir, have experienced difficulties in your own life."

"Yes . . . I have."

"Prejudice and poverty sometimes go hand in hand. I am dedicating my life to eradicating both." He motions for Sherlock to enter the morning room and calls for a servant to bring tea.

Sherlock glances around the room before he sits on a plush black chair with green stripes. Hide sits across from him, while Louise stands behind, looking sullen.

"Mr. Hide, I must say that your home surprises me. I had heard rumors that you came from more humble beginnings."

He chuckles. "Yes, I have heard that said. It must originate from the fact that I speak in the workhouses and soup kitchens, spend most of my time in the East End and Clerkenwell, and try to stand up for those who have little. My family is an old Blackheath one, sir, wealthy, yes. My parents died just a few years ago on an Atlantic crossing to America. I am their only child. They left me this." He glances around the room.

"I am sorry for the loss of your family."

"I thank you for that. My parents were forward-thinking sorts; knew John Stuart Mill and John Bright. Father was a scientist and an inventor. He patented many cures and elixirs, and the profits from such discoveries made us quite comfortable. I was selfish as a youth though, more intrigued by athletics than helping others; was a champion broad jumper at Eton, you know. But their deaths changed me. I wanted to do something that would make them proud. I am attempting to do what I can now, with the talents I have for speaking and political thought, to change our society for the better. As a youth I had wanted to be a scientist, like father, but I am not endowed with his type of brain. Perhaps that is for the better; though I do dabble in the world of chemistry and the like. I have my own laboratory, out back. I gather you are of a scientific turn as well. Would you like to see it?"

How does he know so much about me? Has Louise been feeding him information: If so, why?

Hide gets up and motions for Sherlock to follow him. They pass through a large library. The boy notices Marx's and Engels' names on several spines. The lab door is locked. In fact, it has three or four latches on it. The young man takes several keys out of his pocket. It takes a while, but he gets the locks open. They enter the lab. Sherlock realizes this is the extension at the back of the house. He can see now, that it is almost like a greenhouse: the expansive ceiling is completely made of glass. The room is huge, and many hundreds of test tubes and torts sit on a series of black-topped tables, making Bell's laboratory look modest, indeed. It smells of chemicals, though one odor predominates. *Sulfur.* Sherlock also hears things bubbling and boiling, then notices glass smashed and lying on the floor.

"Oh!" says Hide, looking guilty. "I asked them to clean that up."

There is a knock on the door, but not at the front of the house. It is coming from a small entrance at the rear of the lab.

"Excuse me," says Hide. "There is a gentleman who visits from time to time who, for some reason, likes to use the back door."

Sherlock waits as Hide walks away between the messy tables. The rear door is also locked in several places. *This is a very secretive man.* Finally, Hide gets the door open and speaks to the visitor in hushed tones. Sherlock moves to one side to see better. The man is holding two vials in each hand. He's elderly, eccentrically dressed in a gold cape and wearing a pink skullcap in which something bulges. *Stethoscope.* This strange man is an apothecary. He gives the vials to Hide, who pays him.

"Thank you, Simian."

The man leaves by the same door, Hide locks every latch again, then unlocks a glass cabinet, puts the vials inside and locks it again. He smiles at Sherlock.

"Shall we return to our chairs? It must be getting late . . ." He hesitates, pulls his pocket watch out of his dressing gown, and looks at it. ". . . I have to tell you that I have not been entirely honest with you . . . and I am afraid

I may have to tell you the true reason for Miss Stevenson's visit tonight. I wish I did not."

A grim expression has come across Hide's face. Sherlock feels a jolt of fear pass through his system. *Have I seen something I should not have seen? Is he going to hold me here? Or worse?* He yearns again for his horsewhip.

"Robert," says Louise anxiously as they return, "I must be going. Can you . . . can you give me —"

"Of course, Miss Stevenson — I was just telling Master Holmes that I must explain the exact reason for your coming."

Louise sighs. "Couldn't we just do it in the back room?"

"That wouldn't be polite, not with a guest here, especially a suspicious one." He grins at Sherlock and then shouts for his manservant, asking for a piece of family stationery. When it arrives he walks to a nearby desk and sits down, dipping a pen in an inkwell. The boy spots a stack of papers at his elbow.

"As I said, Master Holmes, I would prefer that you did not know this. No one is aware that I do such things and it is best that way. I am writing a note so Miss Stevenson can take it to my bank and withdraw ten pounds in order to support her family for the next month. That is why she is here . . . if you *must* know. I trust you don't object?"

But Sherlock Holmes isn't thinking about the generosity of Robert Hide, nor does he feel any shame. Something else is suddenly riveting his attention. *Handwriting!* He is remembering that the Jack's handwriting was the same on every note he left behind.

If I can find the hand that wrote those notes, and look up that arm to the face . . . I will have my solution! They weren't written by Louise Stevenson, but here is this well-muscled, dark-haired young man to whom she has just secretly flown, who wants to change England by any means, who speaks of chaos to the masses, who was a champion leaper at Eton, who has made a study of me, who has the smell of sulfur lingering in his lab, whose house is locked at both ends as if he were keeping enormous secrets . . . and he's writing a note!

Sherlock springs to his feet.

Hide regards him. "Master Holmes?"

"A . . . a cramp in my foot. I'm often bothered by them. I just need to stretch it out."

He walks toward Hide. *Perhaps I won't be able to see what he is writing on the note; perhaps it will look too nosey.* He eyes the huge stack of papers on the desk instead. Robert Hide notices, scoops them up, and jams them into a deep drawer.

"I am sorry for the mess, Master Holmes. I tend to write everything down, and then I am left with these piles of rubbish. At every political meeting we have, I insist that we keep notes, minutes, and thorough schedules." He chuckles.

Sherlock smiles back at him. *I have to see what he is writing.* He approaches the desk, glancing from Hide's face, down his arm toward his writing hand. Hide adjusts his position on the chair, almost as if to block Sherlock's view. But Holmes is quick. He pivots and looks over his shoulder.

Robert Hide's handwriting! He imagines rushing to Lestrade, laying it all before him, sending the Force off to Blackheath Village.

TWENTY POUNDS TO THE BEARER OF THIS NOTE.

His heart sinks. *The handwriting is nothing like the Spring Heeled Jack's.*

"Did you not believe me, Master Holmes?" asks Hide genially.

"You, uh . . . you made it out for twenty pounds, not ten."

"Yes, I wish you hadn't seen that either. Mr. Stevenson is truly in need these days."

Louise embraces Hide and thanks him. In moments, she is gone. Hide keeps Sherlock engaged for a long time after she leaves, talking about how he has helped to improve her speech, increasing her vocabulary, reminding her not to drop her *Hs*. He wants her to have more in life. He goes on and on, obviously wanting Louise to have a head start on the boy, so she won't worry about being pursued. But Sherlock has no interest in chasing her. He is feeling terrible. He suspected as good a man as England has, peering over his shoulder when he was secretly giving this poor girl and her family more than she had asked for.

"You are indeed a suspicious young man, Holmes."

"Sometimes, too much so."

"Oh, I don't know. From what I hear of you, I understand you are a brilliant sort, a future detective."

"I doubt that, sir. I may be leaving London soon, to start a new life."

"What a shame. I could use someone with your wits. I'm sure I need not tell you that every day many children starve in this city. And yet, there is enough wealth in

England for all of us to share. The problem is not scarcity, it is greed. I asked Miss Stevenson a good deal about you when she first mentioned you, and I was impressed by what she said. Should you ever want to work with me, I would be glad to employ you."

Sherlock Holmes leaves Blackheath downcast. Because of his success with the Whitechapel murder, the Brixton gang, and the Rathbone kidnapping, he had come to think highly of himself, as if he could solve any crime put before him. But good fortune had obviously been with him. It is indeed ridiculous to think that a boy his age could do what Scotland Yard could not. There had been times when he had thought that before, but now his inadequacy is really sinking in. He is at a dead end. He has absolutely no idea who the Spring Heeled Jack is, not a clue.

He must leave London now, leave Bell, and live in fear that Malefactor will pursue him no matter where he goes. He has been in over his head. He is drowning. He must depart, and try to keep his head above the waves.

18

GOOD-BYES

He doesn't sleep well again that night. In fact, he doesn't sleep at all. His trip home from Blackheath had been harrowing. It had grown dark as he went. Feeling distraught, his confidence diminished, he lost his nerve the minute he was out of the friendly suburbs and into Rotherhithe, unlit as much of it is at night. Malefactor, gone underground, was behind every corner; the Spring Heeled Jack, now a complete mystery to him, was lurking on every building. It was a nightmare. He actually began to run. The Thames Tunnel was the quickest way home, but he didn't dare enter its confines. Instead, he sprinted many miles without stopping, all the way across Blackfriars Bridge, then up through central London to Denmark Street, getting from Southwark to home faster than he had ever made that journey. When he was through the door, he slammed it after him. All was silent. He waited to hear Sigerson Bell's voice, but the old man was either asleep, or out somewhere, probably with his secret clan.

He lies in bed thinking one thing. *I must say good-bye to my father.*

He doesn't wake on Monday morning, he merely gets

up. Bell, of course, has risen early and seems to be in a glorious mood.

"My boy!" he begins, but then sees the haunted look on his young friend. "What . . . why . . ."

"I am leaving."

"Leaving? Leaving what . . . who?"

"You, sir."

The old man blanches. He had been putting on his bright green tweed coat and red fez to go out, but he flops down into a chair with a bang.

Sherlock Holmes owns just the threadbare suit he has on – though he'd been keeping a few shillings in a jar in the lab to buy another – and no other possessions but a second pair of underclothing and socks, and his over-sized nightshirt, which was a hand-me-down gift from his employer. He is now holding them all in his hands. Perhaps the old man will give him a little food to take with him. He doesn't want to offer an explanation of what has happened, but he figures he owes it to the kindly apothecary. It is just occurring to the boy that he must leave school too. He fights back tears. His dreams are shattered.

"But, my young knight, what has happened? I don't think I can allow this!"

In a voice that is barely audible, Sherlock tells him the fix into which the Spring Heeled Jack investigation has put him, and what he now knows about Malefactor, and about Louise Stevenson's visit to Robert Hide, and most importantly, about the note that Master Lestrade found at that horrible crime scene.

When the old man hears about the note, Sherlock thinks he sees a slight expression of suspicion flit across his face, but it doesn't last. It is soon replaced with anger. He leaps to his feet and begins to pace.

"But you cannot have had anything to do with this!" He stops and glances back at Sherlock, "Could you have?"

"No, sir."

"Then we shall save you."

"How, sir?"

The old man is, for the first time since Sherlock has known him, lost for words.

"Well . . . well . . . well . . . well . . . well . . . let me think about it."

"But there is no time, sir. Master Lestrade said he will show the note to his father at noon. He is a good lad and he will likely take his time, give me a few additional hours, but he *must* show it to him. I would do the same – that family was brutally murdered and my name is on the most valuable clue they have. Before the sun sets, the Inspector will know and the Force will come for me."

"They will come here first," nods Bell, "you must leave here, but just for now."

"I must leave here, period."

"No."

"Sir, you always say I should tell the truth, and seek it. You say there are times when we must bow to it." He starts for the door.

"Sherlock!"

Holmes turns back to Sigerson Bell. The old man's eyes are reddening.

"My boy . . . my lad . . . my . . . uh . . . my son. . . . Take these!" The apothecary turns to his cupboards and reaches for a couple of sticks of bread and a bottle of milk and some carrots and onions and jars of stewed fruit and sweets, one after the other, and heaps them into the boy's arms. Then he tosses him a little cloth sack . . . and the horsewhip. He looks like he wants to hug Sherlock as he watches the boy quickly fill the bag with the food and clothes and stuff the whip up a sleeve, but he turns away.

"Go."

"Good-bye, sir . . . and thank you. . . . I . . ."

"Good-bye, Master Sherlock Holmes, keep well."

The boy goes quietly out the door.

About twenty paces down Denmark Street, he hears Bell yelling to him.

"Sherlock!"

The old man is running his way. He has taken off his coat and shoes and even his shirt underneath, as if he had decided to retire to bed, but then remembered something. He's left the red fez on his head. He is naked from the waist up. Pedestrians stop and stare, mouths open; a few women scream. The flesh on his sagging chest hangs down like a dozen thin waves on the sea.

"You mentioned an apothecary at Mr. Hide's. . . . What was his name?"

"Simian."

Bell nods.

"Sir?"

"Farewell," says the old man, and walks back to the shop.

Sherlock is undecided about to whom he should say good-bye. He won't bother with his school. *Irene, his father, Beatrice. No, not Beatrice, just the other two.* His sits on a bench in little Soho Square for a long time, likely a couple of hours, before he can get himself to his feet to do what he must do. He will have to say good-bye for good. The sun is almost directly above. It is nearing noon already.

If he sees Irene first, he can then go to Sydenham to the Crystal Palace. By the time he gets there it will be late afternoon – his father will be in the midst of his duties – Sherlock will at least be well out of London, far to the south. He will then continue in that direction. Perhaps he can walk to Portsmouth, join the Navy, go far away to sea where Lestrade or Malefactor will never find him. It is a good plan.

He heads toward Bloomsbury. *If I had kept my nose out of all of this I would be home now with Mr. Bell, reading a wonderful book from his library, discussing chemistry or litera-ture with him . . . and later there'd be a warm fire, a meal we'd make together.*

When he gets to the Doyle home on Montague Street, he can't bring himself to enter. He hears Irene singing on the floor up above. He can't listen. As he walks away, he hears something else and turns to look at the house. The Corgi, John Stuart Mill, is at a window and has spotted him. He is barking loudly.

Sherlock shuffles off down the street. He makes his way south to the river and over it at London Bridge. It will take him several hours to get to the Crystal Palace so he must keep moving. On Mondays, his father finishes work at 5:00 p.m.

But when he passes The Mint, he can't help stopping. He turns off Borough High Street and walks into his old neighborhood. Will this be the last time he ever sees his family flat above the hatter's shop, where he held his mother in his arms as she died? She had told him that he had much to do in life. . . . *Maybe she meant something other than my silly dream of justice.* He slides against a wall across the little square from the shop and looks up at the top floor. Before long, his eyes drop to ground level. *I have come here to see Beatrice, not the flat.* Miss Leckie is almost a perfect human being – kind and gentle, but brave and intelligent and . . . he will admit, very beautiful. She is beautiful both inside and out. He must also admit that he feels drawn to her; very much so. Now, when he compares her to Irene Doyle, he sees how much more there is to this lowly hatter's daughter. She has no airs. People too often judge others by their outsides, the cut of their clothing, and their friends. He has known Miss Leckie almost since they were born. It is as if she were meant for him. Miss Doyle is from another world. What did Louise Stevenson say? *"Beatrice is a fine soul – finer than any of us – who cares for you, Master Holmes . . . though I'm not sure why."* No truer words were ever spoken. Will he ever know anyone like her again?

He sits there, not caring who sees him slumped on the foot pavement. A few locals recognize him, try to engage him – Ratfinch the fishmonger rolls his eel cart past and attempts to get him to rise – but he waves them all off. It begins to grow darker. He must get up and go to Sydenham. He will hide there in a field somewhere and say good-bye to his father in the morning. Young Lestrade will have shown the note to his father by now. The Inspector will already have the Force searching the streets for him. They will come here. In fact, they are likely on their way.

He rises. He notices a dim light flickering on in the hatter's shop, their only gas lamp, or perhaps it's a candle. *I must take this chance, do what is right, see her, and tell her, at least, that I admire her. I owe her that.* He walks to the shop and knocks gently on the door.

Her father answers. His cloudy red eyes look more tired than ever, and his meaty round face appears as though it has begun to shrink. In the old days, it was often set in a scowl, but he wasn't, and isn't, an angry man, just serious and dedicated to his trade. He has had to work without stopping for many years to keep himself and Beatrice alive. He dearly loves his daughter.

The sales part of the shop with its counter and hat trees is dark. Over Mr. Leckie's shoulder, through a door left ajar, Sherlock sees light coming from the living quarters. Sitting at a table in there, leaning over something with a pen in hand, is Beatrice. There is a fire on in the room – the light the boy had seen flicker. Sherlock gazes at her, barely hearing Mr. Leckie.

"Ah, Master 'olmes. It is a pleasure to see you again, sir. You will forgive me. I was lying down on me little bed

'ere behind the counter to let Miss Beatrice do up some correspondence. I need me rest these days, me mind gets tired.
She works so 'ard, she does, but keeps up the letters to our
folks and friends, too. Why are you carrying that sack, sir?"

"May I see her?"

"Yes . . . yes, Master 'olmes. Just go through. She is
always 'appy to see you. I'll just lie down 'ere again. Won't
bother you two young folk."

Sherlock walks silently across the dark room, avoiding
the hats hanging from hooks. When he gets close to the
door, he stops and simply looks at her. Her head is bent
down and she is writing carefully, thinking about what she
is saying. She seems to be pressing the pen down hard onto
the paper. Her bonnet is off and her long black hair hangs
in ringlets almost onto the paper. There is a little wooden
box on the table near her hand. Because she is next to
the fire, she isn't wearing a shawl. In fact, she has pulled the
sleeves of her dress up, so her slender forearms and wrists are
visible. Sherlock beams. A wonderful idea comes to his
mind. *In my new life, I can have a partner. There would be
none better than Beatrice Leckie, and I know she would choose
me too. Perhaps, in a few years, I can send for her. What if we
talk about it . . . tonight.*

He pushes the door and it creaks. Beatrice turns with
a smile, but when she sees who it is she gasps and puts her
hand to her mouth.

"Sherlock!" The look of fear dissolves into happiness.
But there is something else there too. *Guilt.* Instantly, she
turns to her writing and stuffs the paper into her dress pocket.

The boy drops his cloth sack on the floor. "Doing your correspondence?"

"Yes . . . yes, I like to write at night."

"The way you put your letter away when I came . . . it must be very private. I suppose you are writing to someone special. Perhaps I should go." His heart is sinking. *Why would I assume that Beatrice Leckie has no one special in her life? There were many boys at school who liked her.*

Beatrice sees his intent. "Oh, no! No, Sherlock, it isn't like that!"

"That is fine, Beatrice. I was just going, anyway."

"Sherlock!" she rises and takes him by the hand. "Don't go. I'll . . . I'll show you what I would write . . . if I were writing to you."

She takes another piece of paper from a sideboard nearby, leans over it with a coquettish smile, hiding its contents from the boy. She writes. The ink is red. She hands it to him, glowing up.

"I LOVE YOU," it says.

But Sherlock isn't smiling back. There is a shiver going down his spine. And it isn't pleasurable. *Her handwriting! It is EXACTLY the same as the Spring Heeled Jack's!*

He seizes her. For an instant, she thinks he is trying to embrace her. But he has her by the arms and is pulling her to her feet, hard.

"Sherlock! You're 'urting me!"

"You wrote those notes! YOU!"

"Please let me go!"

He pins her to the table and reaches into her dress, fishing out the notes from her pocket. She wrests one arm free and holds it over the little wooden box on the table, as if to keep the lid down. Sherlock wrenches that arm off and almost in the same motion, flicks open the lid. There is a stack of papers inside. He sees two words written in red across the one on top, same handwriting, TREASURE FAMILY, and then some numbers and a word he can't read. Struggling to hold her, he flicks it and sees the note underneath. MUST HAVE it says, but the rest is ripped. He sees the word CHAOS! on another note under that.

"A family was murdered!" he shouts at her. He can feel tears coming to his eyes, but he won't let her go. He digs deeper into her pocket. She sinks her nails into his hand, but he pulls out all the papers. There are three of them, one with writing, the other two blank. She reaches out and claws at him, but he throws her to the floor. He spreads the notes on the table.

"Beatrice?" Her father has risen from his bed and is coming toward the door.

MARCH 10 reads the first note and two addresses in Lambeth. He recognizes them as poor areas.

"What does this mean?"

On the floor, Beatrice is crying. "Sherlock, please don't! You won't understand!"

March 10 is tomorrow.

"WHAT DOES THIS MEAN?"

"I can't tell you!" she cries.

A startled Mr. Leckie is now at the door. "What is going on in here?" he asks.

It's a schedule. It's tomorrow's locations for the fiend's attacks! It is growing dark outside. The police will be coming . . . the villain is about to prowl. *What about tonight? Where is he scheduled to strike tonight?*

"Who is the Spring Heeled Jack, Beatrice? WHO IS HE!"

"Don't . . . don't ask me," she cries, putting her hands to her head. "I can't tell you, Sherlock."

Mr. Leckie grips the tall boy and tries to knock him to the floor. "I can't allow this! Why is you asking 'er this? What is you up to? Is you this fiend, Sherlock 'olmes!"

"Let him go, father!" shouts Beatrice, getting to her feet and pulling him away from the boy. "He means no harm."

"Oh, yes, I do, Miss Leckie! I mean harm to anyone who means harm to others. And you are one of those!"

"No, Sherlock!"

"You were writing up the schedule for planned assaults for tomorrow night!"

"No!"

She wrote the notes that were left on the victims, in order to protect the Jack, in her girlish hand so the handwriting could never be traced to him. Very clever. But what about these schedules? For some reason, she was asked to make them up. Why? Is she the mastermind? Does the Jack want everything written down? If so, he's an amateur – it leaves a trail. Are the notes sent by mail? Then he doesn't live nearby.

"Tell me one thing and save your soul, Beatrice Leckie. Tell me where he will strike tonight!"

She sobs, holding her father, and says nothing.

"Tell me!"

"I can't! I just can't!"

He turns back to the notes on the table. He remembers how hard she was pressing with the ink pen, making big, thick letters. He looks at the first of the two blank notes beneath. *She must sit here at night and plan for attacks in different parts of London, moving things around to keep the police guessing – eluding them. She must have done this last night too! Then she sends them to the Jack!* He picks up a blank paper and sees a faint outline of letters, impressed into the page. He can make out the words MARCH 10. *That came from writing today's note.* He picks up the other blank sheet. The trace of handwriting is very faint. *This must have been made yesterday! It will have today's attacks on it!* But he can't read it. He steps toward the fire.

"NO!" shouts Beatrice and tries to grab his arm.

He snatches the sheet away and holds it close to the flames. The impression becomes visible.

MARCH 9 – ONE APPEARANCE – OLD NICHOL STREET ROOKERY, BETHNAL GREEN

Crying, Beatrice is hugging him now, as if he were as dear to her as a husband. He shoves her away, picks up the notes from the table and the box, and leaving his cloth sack behind, runs out the door and into the street.

"HOLMES!"

It is Inspector Lestrade. He is just down the street, rushing toward the hatter's shop, three Bobbies by his side. Several feet behind, as if reluctant to be part of this, is his son.

Sherlock is off like a shot, and they are immediately after him. But he has run through the twisting and turning arteries of The Mint since he was a little child, and within minutes, he has lost them. He takes them south. Now, he doubles back and heads north, making for London Bridge. He tries not to think of Beatrice Leckie, his "flawless friend" . . . in league, somehow, with this violent fiend. *Trust no one.* Malefactor was right.

The Old Nichol Street Rookery in Bethnal Green is a perfect site for another Spring Heeled Jack attack. Beatrice and whomever she is working with have made a smart decision. It is north of the river and almost all the other appearances have been to the south. It is also in a poor neighborhood, *very* poor – just above Whitechapel Road in the East End. The Old Nichol Street Rookery is a London slum unlike any other, infamous for its crowded conditions, its crime and disease. But Sherlock runs across the bridge toward it, heading for it like a racehorse. He *knows* where the Spring Heeled Jack is about to strike! He will confront him in the dangerous little streets and alleys of that desperate slum amidst its filth and poverty. It would be best to be accompanied by others, by young Lestrade, by the Force themselves. But that is impossible. His only hope of staying in London, staying with Sigerson Bell, and becoming the person he wants to be, is to do this alone, completely alone. *Alone is best anyway. I can't believe I thought of Beatrice Leckie as a partner!*

If he can capture the Jack, or at least set up a hue and cry and attract the police, all will be well. They will see that he is the Jack's enemy, not his accomplice. *But who is this fiend? Who is working with Beatrice Leckie? Can I REALLY confront him? This villain seems to have almost supernatural powers.*

Holmes is glad he has his horsewhip up his sleeve.

19

As he runs, he thinks. But his mind keeps turning to Beatrice. *How could she do this?* He shirks it off. *Think about the crimes. What do I know?* He considers the note that young Lestrade found in the Isle of Dogs. *It had horse hairs on it . . . the blood was a strange color. What if the blood, all that blood saturating the marsh, was actually horse blood?*

He runs up through the old city, toward Bethnal Green. His heart is pumping and not just due to the strain of his sprint. The neighborhoods are getting worse. Darkness has now completely descended. Even if Beatrice wanted to help him, she couldn't – young Lestrade will have stopped at the hatter's shop.

The crowds are thin at this hour, but he senses that someone is following him, far back among the pedestrians. *Malefactor?* The young crime lord has gone underground, but Sherlock knows that he will never be free of the scoundrel. *I am vulnerable while I am pursuing someone else, my attention on my prey.*

But then he feels a second presence, up high on the buildings. Sherlock is scurrying along wide Shoreditch

Road, in order to keep off the smaller streets for as long as possible. He glances back and up onto the roofs . . . *no one.*

He turns to his task again, running, thinking once more of Beatrice's notes, now stuffed in his pockets. *She wrote the Treasure family's name on one!* He can't bear to even imagine her involved in what that fiend did. Huffing and puffing, he pulls that note from his pocket with a sweaty hand and looks at it closely. *The date and the time are for tomorrow. But the Isle of Dogs murder occurred yesterday. It doesn't make sense. There is another word written there –* MONTREAL. *Why Montreal? What does that mean?* He contemplates another note, the one with the strange message: MUST HAVE. It was smaller than the others and ripped after the letter E. The note young Lestrade had found at the crime scene said SHERLOCK HOLMES ON OUR SIDE. It was ripped too, right before his name. *What if you put them together?* MUST HAVE SHERLOCK HOLMES ON OUR SIDE. The fiend must have had that note with him! But, perhaps as he struggled with his victims, as he did his gruesome deed, it was pulled from his pocket . . . ripped in two, and left on the ground. Aware that something incriminating remained at the scene, Beatrice searched the area and found one half. *But why was that maniac carrying the note in the first place? Why did he want ME on his side? Or did Beatrice?*

He is nearing Bethnal Green. Again, he senses that two figures are pursuing him, one on the ground and one up above. Darting around a corner, he stops. No one comes.

He reaches Church Street, and turns into big Bethnal Green Road. The rookery is in there, a few strides up

Church and then to the left. He can actually smell it. It is renowned for it odors – human refuse in pools, slaughter houses, the boiling entrails and fat of animals, used by the rich for dog food, but here for human sustenance. Drunks lie about on the small streets. Herds of families live together in bedraggled, broken-down buildings. Tradesman, dustmen, costermongers, and silkweavers live mostly on its exterior, leaving the rotting core to criminals, prostitutes, and the desperately poor. John Bright often cries out for the Old Nichol Street Rookery in his speeches. "England," he says, "has forgotten one of its children: ugly, diseased, forsaken; the East End of the East End."

Sherlock Holmes has never been inside this rookery. He can feel his knees shaking. He turns down Church and then left onto a smaller road. He can hear people screaming, babies crying, their little voices hoarse. At first, he sees no one. Then he comes to Old Nichol Street itself. The buildings are short and skinny, made of brick or stone, or of tumble-down rotting wood; many doors are wide open. It is nearly pitch-dark, not a single gas lamp evident. On the cobblestones, the scene is revolting. A row of children, ten or so in number, lie almost naked on the filthy road among piles and pools of animal and human refuse. Fast asleep, some are so still that they may be dead. A pig snorts near them, a hag is shrieking from a little window at an unseen foe. The smell is overpowering. It almost turns Sherlock's stomach. He hears the sound of footsteps echoing in the distance, and looking down the street, he can make out three shadowy men chasing a girl, a "lady of the night," though she is dressed like anything but a lady. The boy can tell from where he stands that her long hair hangs in sweaty clumps, likely filled with lice, her cotton dress is stained and ripped and torn. She is in bare feet. As they near, he sees the terror on her face. She is dark-haired, like Beatrice, dark-eyed like her too; in her fearful grimace he sees missing teeth. The men are shouting now, and she is screaming. She is clutching something in her hand. Perhaps a coin, maybe a morsel of food: something they want? This poor young prostitute is Beatrice's age, just fourteen or fifteen. She sees Sherlock and reaches out for him. He can see – through the grime – that she might have been as beautiful as Beatrice, had life been different for her. His former friend, but for her job and meager education, could *be* this girl, running for her life in the Nichol Street Rookery.

"Help me!" she cries.

At that very moment, a bat-like figure appears above them on the only building of any height on the street – a two-storey stone edifice, the words *Jackel, Butcher* imprinted in chipped letters on the front.

"CHAOS!" it shrieks.

Sherlock looks up and freezes. It spreads its wings. It is about to leap, all the way to the ground; its target . . . the girl. The villains in pursuit of her freeze too. Then the Spring Heeled Jack spots Sherlock Holmes. He turns to him. *That face.* It looks like someone he knows. But it isn't him. *It can't be!* The expression is distorted, the eyes red, veins pop out on the forehead, the hair is disheveled, sticking up in places like devil's ears, and when it speaks a blue flame ushers from its mouth. But most disconcerting are the eyes. They look down at the boy with evil glee, a disturbed intent, as if the mind behind them is as mad as the worst lunatic in the Bethnal Green Asylum.

"SHERLOCK HOLMES!" it cries. Then it descends.

Just as it is about to crush him, Sherlock hears footsteps smacking toward him, *clop-clop* on the cobblestones like a racehorse down the stretch . . . and catches sight of Sigerson Bell coming at him out of the corner of his eye. His face is distorted too, devilry in it. *He is in on it after all*, thinks Sherlock – *trust no one*. Bell leaps, a long, fantastic leap, and in midflight, strikes the boy right in the chest. Sherlock hits the cobblestones, and all the air is driven from his lungs. He lies there beneath the bizarre apothecary, gasping for air, feeling like he is dying. He looks up into the cold black London sky. There are no stars, of course. Beside them, the Jack has struck the hard ground without the anticipated cushion of the boy's body. But it doesn't seem to care. It rolls and leaps to its feet. Sherlock expects Bell to get off him and allow the Jack to have him, to hand him over. But the old man speaks into his ear at break-neck speed.

"You have merely suffered a winding of the upper respiratory system. Relax, and the air shall return and proper functioning of the lungs will ensue."

Relax? thinks Sherlock.

"Stay on the ground, my boy. I shall attend to this fiend."

As he finishes, Bell springs to his feet, spins on a needlehead . . . and confronts the Spring Heeled Jack! Down below, head on the stones, not a breath of air in his entire body, Sherlock Holmes actually smiles.

"KEE-AAHH!" screams Bell.

The girl stands back in amazement. A bent-over man, at least a hundred years old in her estimation, wearing tight and nearly transparent leggings and an oriental bandana around his head, has assumed a fighting stance within a few feet of the powerfully built villain, the most feared and evil man in London. Bell turns his hips and powers a punch toward the Jack's head. But the fiend is quick. He ducks slightly and catches the blow on the meat of his shoulder. Then he turns on the old man. Blue flames stream from his mouth again.

"Sulfur," says Bell, just as the Spring Heeled Jack pivots on a leg, raises the other, and thrusts a kick into his opponent, using the sole of his big, black boot flat across the old man's scrawny chest. The sound is like a gun going off. Bell flies halfway across the street and slams into a stone wall.

"Rat flatulence!"

The air completely leaves his lungs, and he falls to the ground and lies still. The Jack walks forward and stands above him, laughing.

On the stones nearby, Sherlock feels a wisp of air enter his upper body. He shakes his arm and lets the horsewhip fall from his sleeve, into his hand. The Jack is facing away from him. He struggles to his knees, pulls the whip back, snaps it in the air and cracks it at the villain. Just as intended, it wraps around his legs. Holmes jerks it violently, pulling his target off his feet, way up into the air. The fiend lands on his face on the hard road surface without getting his hands down for protection.

But he is apparently indestructible – he immediately rises, kicking off the whip. There is blood on his face. He advances on Sherlock and glares down at the boy, just a few feet away.

It's him!

"Please turn somewhat, about forty-five degrees," says a high-pitched voice. The expression on the Jack's face indicates that he knows it is the old man who has spoken and that he is now standing behind him. Still, he doesn't see the Bellitsu kick coming. As the fiend turns his head just so – forty-five degrees – exposing his left temple, Bell's foot connects with it at a top speed, perfectly, according to the rules of physics. London's most feared villain is unconscious before he hits the ground.

"A patient taught me how to recover from a winding of the respiratory system in less then five point seven-five seconds. It has to do with the relaxation of the anal sphincter and –"

"Uh sir?"

"Yes, my boy?"

"I don't think we need to know that, not right now."

"Quite. More pertinent would be getting this chap hog-tied and delivered to Scotland Yard."

Sherlock Holmes turns the unconscious Spring Heeled Jack onto his back. Robert Hide's face is still distorted.

"It barely looks like him," says the boy.

"Sherlock!" They turn and see Beatrice Leckie and

young Lestrade run into Old Nichol Street and hurry toward the scene. Bell turns back to the fallen man.

"Well, it isn't him in a sense, my young knight. It is his double. When you mentioned the name of the apothecary, I knew something was not right with Robert Hide. Simian is a practitioner who dabbles in the dark arts. He went over to the shadowy side long ago. Most apothecaries try to help others bring health and goodness and progress of the human spirit to the world . . . then, there are others. I believe one of those vials you saw Simian giving Hide contained a substance removed from the reproductive parts of an aggressive male animal – perhaps a baboon or an ape. The other likely contained secretions from the glands that adjoin the tops of human kidneys."

"Aggressive male animal?" asks Beatrice, as the other two arrive.

"Why that's Robert Hide!" exclaims young Lestrade.

"Apothecaries have long believed that there are chemicals within males that make us manly," continues Bell, "a powder keg of elements for the male arsenal, if you will. If one could find a way to multiply that supply, then ignite it with secretions from those glands that impart vigor to our systems, someone could possess energy almost beyond his control. A man could become a triple man! And the dark personality inside would be free to come forth . . . creating a fiend!"

"We didn't agree to 'is doing anything like that," says Beatrice.

"We?" asks Lestrade.

"I went to Blackheath tonight and waited outside Hide's house," says Bell. "I wanted to catch that Simian rat red-handed. But as it got dark, I saw a figure through the glass in Hide's laboratory. He appeared to be putting on a costume. When I saw the wings, it did not take me long to comprehend what that costume was. Then I watched his shadow take the vials from the cabinet and ingest them. He stood still for a moment. Then he staggered, and his shadow transformed. It seemed to grow before my eyes. He began smashing bottles and test tubes in the laboratory. Then he leapt, in a single bound from a squat on the floor up onto a counter. In moments he was rushing out the door and coming this way. He took to the rooftops once he got to the north side of the river, ran along them, and when there were spaces between the buildings, he jumped . . . sometimes more than ten feet at a time!"

"'e must have been fortifying 'imself," says Beatrice, looking down at him with sympathy. "It wasn't in 'is nature to be so violent. 'e must have felt that 'e 'ad to . . . be someone else to do this. 'e had to use the devil inside. We didn't know."

"We?" says Lestrade again. "Beatrice, how can you know anything about this? You told me we were coming here to see Master Holmes . . . that he would be in trouble."

"I have been 'elping the Spring 'eeled Jack."

"You what?"

"She and Louise Stevenson and Robert Hide concocted the first attack," says Sherlock. "They did it late at night when there wouldn't be enough witnesses to intervene, just a few who might report it, give it credence when, as they hoped, it got into the papers. They played it out, screams included, exactly as if the Jack were a real villain and they real victims."

"Robert Hide," says Beatrice, looking down at him, "would give 'is life for people like my father and me, and Louise and 'er poor family. 'e was excited about the changes that Mr. Disraeli had made and said that when a Conservative prime minister can do such things – give the vote to many millions at the stroke of 'is pen – the politicians must be at the point where they would make more changes. 'e said they would surely do almost anything to keep the peace . . . if their 'ands were forced. Robert thought now was the time to strike for the poor, for children, for women. 'e said we needed to create fear in the streets." She looks sad. "The idea of the return of the Spring 'eeled Jack came to us."

"You told him that you could get me involved, didn't you?"

"Yes, but it was in the cause of good, in the end, Sherlock. I told 'im that I knew a boy, a brilliant boy, a wonderful boy, who believed in justice. I knew you 'ad 'elped the police capture some of the worst criminals in London over the past year. But the public didn't know. I told him that the senior Inspector at Scotland Yard was jealous of you – 'ated you."

"That is, perhaps, too strong a word," mutters young Lestrade.

"Let us tell the truth, sir," says Bell.

"But I told Robert," continues Beatrice, "that you would never agree to 'elping us, that you would think our plan reckless and criminal. So, we came up with a way to make you 'elp us without you knowing. And we enlisted Master Lestrade as well."

"No, you didn't."

"Yes, we did."

"Women, Sherlock," says Bell. "You see, they are not what they seem. Oh, excuse me. Miss Leckie, do go on. You were explaining how you deceived these young men so easily."

She gives him a look, but continues.

"We never intended to 'urt anyone. It was the opposite. We thought a sense of chaos would push the government to *really* 'elp people in need. But we knew that a simple Spring 'eeled Jack appearance, even several of them, would be treated as pranks, nothing more. We thought if we could involve Sherlock 'olmes, the boy whom the lead inspector at Scotland Yard 'ated, get him to pursue the case, and make sure Lestrade knew he was doing so . . . then the Force would go after it with everything they 'ad and the public would know that. Fear would grow. Louise and I, we know London, we know where the poor are, we live like them ourselves. Robert, for all his brilliance and understanding, doesn't. So it was us who scheduled his appearances and moved them around London. In order to protect 'im, should he be suspected . . . I wrote the notes he left behind. Every few days I wrote up 'is locations and 'is notes to leave at the crime scene, and 'ad them delivered to Blackheath. Louise and I, we tried to stay away from 'im, so no one could connect us. And every day, I fed the press everything I could."

"But . . ." gasps Lestrade, "you were involved in the murder of an entire family! Hide turned into a beast! You are an accomplice to a gruesome butchery!" His eyes are turning red. He reaches out and takes her violently by the arm. But Sherlock pulls him off.

"There was no murder. No one was injured by this Spring Heeled Jack . . . unless you count the self-inflicted wounds on Miss Leckie."

Beatrice looks ashamed.

"No murder? What do you mean?"

"Horse blood, my friend: all that blood was horse blood."

"So where are the bodies? Where is the Treasure family, those little girls?"

"They are upright and healthier than ever, probably living somewhere in Mr. Hide's large home. They were his followers, friends of his who believed in him."

"Yes," says Beatrice.

"They are scheduled to leave London tomorrow by boat," continues Sherlock, "for a better life in Montreal, in Canada." He turns to his childhood friend. "I have only one question. Why was Hide carrying the note about me?"

"He wasn't."

"I beg your pardon?"

"I planted it on the scene afterward, for Master Lestrade to find."

"You what?" says Lestrade.

"You still weren't 'elping us, Sherlock. I had to MAKE you. I know you, and I guessed you wouldn't give in. I did what I 'ad to do."

"But why a note ripped in two?"

"Because if they caught you, if you were really in trouble, I was going to bring the other part to police head-quarters . . . and give myself up."

Sherlock has to steel himself. "I didn't calculate that properly," he says weakly.

"Whatever your theories are, Master Holmes," says Lestrade, glaring down at Robert Hide, "I want this fiend bound by hand and foot like the pig he is! You shall all stay here with him while I send word to my father! You, Miss Leckie, and Miss Stevenson, shall be taken to Scotland Yard and brought before the magistrates for aiding and abetting –"

"What?" interrupts Sherlock.

"A . . . a . . ."

"A Penny Dreadful character?"

"Who –"

"Who committed the crime of scaring people, in order to make England a better place?"

Lestrade has no immediate response.

"When he comes to," says Sherlock, "let him go."

"No! I cannot allow this!"

"With this proviso . . . that he arranges for the sale of his property and follows the Treasure family to Canada, where he will never use terror to do what is right. If he stays here, your father, indeed, must arrest him."

"But –"

Holmes puts his hand on Lestrade's shoulder. The older boy sighs, then nods.

"Thank you," says Beatrice. She is glowing at Sherlock again, and her eyes are watering. She reaches out to him.

He pulls away. "Miss Leckie, you were playing with fire. I would advise you too, if you seek to do good in this world, to never use fear or terror to do so."

"Like you?" she asks, giving him a hardened look. "No, you would *never* do anything unsavory to bring about justice, would you?"

"Best not to answer that, my boy," says Bell.

But Sherlock has turned away from her, to Lestrade, "Give your father this." He reaches into a pocket, pulls out the two halves of the ripped note and hands them over. "And assure him that the threat of the Spring Heeled Jack has been taken care of. Should he have any questions, he knows where to find me."

A big grin spreads over the apothecary's face.

The poor girl in the stained dress, with the greasy hair and gap-toothed smile has been forgotten in all of this. She is looking down at the fiend who intended to attack her. He is beginning to groan and stir. She smiles at him.

"Thank you," she says.

20

THE MAN

Sherlock walks home alone that night, despite Sigerson Bell's objections. The boy knows he won't be able to sleep anyway. He wants to be on Westminster Bridge. When he gets there, he ignores the stragglers, the prostitutes, the drunks, who stagger in circles behind him and make rude talk. He even ignores the possibility that somewhere in the shadows, Malefactor may be watching him. Instead, he leans over the balustrade where Beatrice and Louise and Robert Hide enacted their dramatic scene.

Despite his triumph, he is feeling sad. He knows he must always be wary of slipping into deep, dark moods, but he feels one coming on.

How could she have done what she did? But it was for good, wasn't it? Isn't she still a remarkable person? Isn't Irene? He isn't sure. He looks up at Big Ben. *Trust no one. But shouldn't we all do the opposite – trust one another, care for each other? Are we capable of that? We all have a secret fiend inside.*

He steps away from the wall and walks toward Westminster Palace. Up ahead, he sees a beautiful four-wheeled carriage moving very slowly along the street, the liveried coachman holding the reins tightly . . . and a man walking beside it. His dark suit looks expensive but somehow ill-fitting; and though he seems rather elderly, his tall top hat sits on a big head with black curly hair hanging down, so black it looks as if it were dyed. He walks with a slight stoop, deep in contemplation, his gleaming walking stick tapping out each step. Sherlock nears. Then his heart almost stops.

Disraeli.

The prime minister of the British Empire is fifteen strides in front of him: this great man, this Jew, unique in history – a popular novelist and dandy in his youth, now the most powerful man on earth, who rose through genius and courage, despite the prejudice against him . . . who gave a quarter of England, after two thousand years, their democratic rights. Sherlock feels as though he may faint. Instead, he darts across the road.

"You avoid me, young man? Am I not fit to speak to?" says a low voice.

Sherlock comes to a halt. So does the carriage.

"The prime minister wishes your presence," says the coachman.

The boy turns and walks slowly back across the road, his head lowered.

"Look at me, son."

The aging visage, wrinkled from work and care, still has those dark, twinkling eyes, that big nose the political illustrators like to exaggerate, as if he were a Hebrew Pinocchio, as if he were Mr. Dickens' evil Jew, Fagin. For

Sherlock Holmes, looking at him is like looking into the face of God.

"You are about the streets at a rather late hour."

"So . . . so are you, sir."

The prime minister lets out a huge guffaw.

"Oh! I do not get to laugh much anymore."

"Sir . . . why can we not all vote: women and men and all the poor?"

"Ah. You are a thinker. That is good." He pats Sherlock on the shoulder. The boy wonders if he will ever clean that spot again. "When I was a youth I was impetuous. I wanted to be the greatest novelist the world had ever seen and the choice of all the ladies *and* the fanciest dresser. And when I first became a politician, I wanted to change the world . . . on my first day in parliament!"

Sherlock smiles.

"But humanity will not put up with that. We are a rather large group with many points of view. There will always be poverty, hatred, poisonous ideas, as well as love and kindness and decency. Life changes slowly. The most important thing is to do your part to *steer* things in the right direction. And that is what I am trying to do. Like my fellow human beings, I am not always right . . . I am not always good. I have a bad side. We all do. I have, for example, a very poor opinion of my *scandalous* opponent . . . Mr. Gladstone, and I use the term *Mr.* with some reservation. But I am trying, I have my nose, this big Jewish nose, pointed, I think, in the right direction. And with me, I hope to take the English people. Some day, we will, indeed, *all* vote."

"I am a Jew," blurts out the boy.

"Are you? What is your name?"

"Sherlock Holmes."

"Well, Master Holmes, if you might allow me to impart some advice, do not be too much of a Jew. Be a human being first. Treasure your Jewishness, but listen to others – they may be, believe it or not, just as noble as you. That's what the Christians must do – and the Muslims and the Conservatives and the Liberals and the Irish, who are igniting bombs in our city to get their way, and the Americans, who so often think they are right when they have no idea, and cause damage in the world."

Benjamin Disraeli pauses and sighs.

"This Spring Heeled Jack chap, he who wants to scare us into change – his terror will not work, I assure you. We shall change, together, at our own speed. He is of the mistaken impression that what he believes is the truth . . . and all others are wrong. It is good to have beliefs, do not misunderstand me. But if you think you are absolutely right about something, my son, about anything . . . then you probably aren't. Human beings are not God. We were cast out from the Garden of Eden when we tried to be. We are all imperfect, but if we are wise, we learn every day. Tell me, what are you going to do with your life?"

"My mother was killed by a criminal. I want to seek justice. But I can't, not yet. I am still just a boy."

"Nonsense!" shouts the prime minister. He glares at the lad, sending a shiver right into his heart. "BEGIN TODAY!" Disraeli turns away. He taps his stick on his carriage and gingerly climbs in. It starts to pull away.

"I am counting on you, Sherlock Holmes," he says, as the coachman urges the horses past the Palace of Westminster, into the London night. Up above, Big Ben strikes midnight.

**Be sure to read the first three books
in the award-winning series:**

EYE OF THE CROW

DEATH IN THE AIR

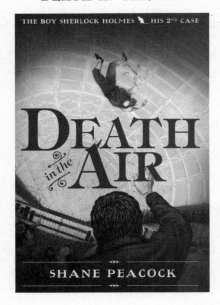

VANISHING GIRL

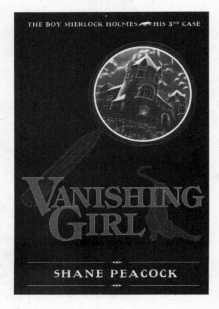